fisher of men

by

bradley f koetting

FISHER OF MEN by Bradley F. Koetting

Copyright © 2008 by Bradley Fredrick Koetting

Single Malt Press

PO Box 43

Timberon, New Mexico 88350-0034

bfkoetting@gmail.com

Also by Bradley F. Koetting: *running out of fear,*
push buttons & stir pots

ISBN - 978-0-615-25619-1

ACKNOWLEDGMENTS

thank you

my Lord and Savior, Jesus Christ, God, the Father Almighty, Mom, Pop & MeeMaw, Sug, Goat, Tom, Marfa Kdub, Mr.Pink, David and Shawn, Cleat, Camie Joe, Betsy, Ted and Granny, Betty and the family, Kerr and Mary Bell, all the ranches, Poopy Doo, Poopy Doo II, and soon to be Poopy Doo III, Doc Allen, Terry, Yolie, The Troglodyte, Talkin Andrew, Roy, Mr. Card, Lee, Chris, Pito, C-Shot, Stephen Barry Frankoff, Terry, Lancifer, Dawn, Lindsey, Greg, Chip, Kevin, Bob and Kevin, Anita, Laura, Eve, Chavez, Charlie, Townes, Guy, Blaze, Joe, Butch, Terry, Robert Earl, the Carrizal, Servando, Herky, Joseph Bradley Broussard, Bret Broussard, Erick and Carlos, Morris L. West, Lanman, US and the entire Fish Camp crew, the Jax boys, Mem and Jeanne, Mongo, Marla, Billy Dale, Trixie, Marty, Julian, Joel, Jimmy, Houston Kdub, Paul, Kelly, The Big Guy, my sweet Billie Bear, Joe, Juanita and the kids, Dr. Solcher, Dr. Lynch, Dr. Luecke, Dr. Sampson, Maurie and all the other kind, gentle nurses all over Texas, Scotty, Wolfgang, Maxwell, Abby and Azle, Boot, Mantequilla, Siete Leguas, Park Ranger Paul, all the real cowboys and cowgirls, Dogman, 'Big Son, The', and all of the other angels – wings or not.

for Mister John

"...yesterday I met a whole man. It is a rare experience, but always an illuminating and ennobling one. It costs so much to be a full human being that there are very few who have the enlightenment, or the courage, to pay the price... One has to abandon altogether the search for security and reach out to the risk of living with both arms. One has to embrace the world like a lover, and yet demand no easy return of love. One has to accept pain as a condition of existence. One has to court doubt and darkness as the cost of knowing. One needs a will stubborn in conflict, but apt always to the total acceptance of every consequence of living and dying."

Morris L. West
The Shoes of a Fisherman

without passion it is not life
and fate is faith's only challenge

The only line that I had written in months lay over my sleeping eyes like a broken stone. I was thinking of people when I wrote it. How they fascinated me with their particulars. And those that just passed me by because their world seemed so real and connected and outside my own. I thought first of the ones who made me laugh, then the smart ones, and then the odd ones – the people that just do their thing. These were the ones that truly intrigued me. They drown in passion, and they never die. They do good for the world during their time there. Capitulation to passion brings peace to man. That's the only bright side of surrender. Otherwise there should never be surrender – ever.

My fascination with existence had simply become too much. My mind strained not to burst when I contemplated the grand scale of things. There's irony gleaming in the ardent life of humankind: we're only dying with the tedious unwinding of eternity. The earth was where I lived. It was my home for a while. It demanded my time, my love and my life. My life. Mine and mine alone. And as I imagined it, so to me it came – taking me from the warm black cloud of oblivion and into the teeth of that foul, beloved humanity.

Then the damn phone rang. It was just past four in the morning. I climbed out of a drunken sleep and reached over a soft, warm body. The room was dark and humid and still. Moonlight filtered in off the bay and lay in the air like fog. It was much too early to be awake after so much wine. My head ached and throbbed. My mouth dry, layered thick with warm cotton or sand or shit or all of it together frappe-like. An overwhelmingly strong, viciously controlling hangover. Normally I was fortunate enough to sleep through this stage of it, but not that night. It was the irresistible taste of a bone-dry cabernet that did it to me. One glass with a pretty girl, and the blood would flow and flow until there was no more or the sex began or I passed out. I referred to it as blood because it was my blood. It was more my blood than my blood was my blood, and I didn't see this as any particular problem. Lucky for me I was in America, and I could do as I pleased and was pleased to be doing it without any consequential regard. Single malt scotch, too. Though it did make me a bit aggressive, we always had a strong attraction to one another – whiskey and me.

I was exhausted and dirty from all the sex. My room smelled like sex. Stale, hard, finished sex. The old ceiling fan had finally given out a few nights prior. I was just getting used to sleeping without it. Uncomfortable and nauseous, my skin burned from deep inside. Too much wine and already, in a sudden moment of uninvited sobriety, I felt the world flaming to life inside me.

"Hello." My voice, coarse and dry. It reminded me of the cigarettes and how I smoked sometimes when I drank, but I had no desire when I was sober. Smokes can be a very effective drinking regulator, only they regulate a constant flow of alcohol and more cigarettes and nothing else. Oddly, I was not indifferent to smoking on occasion, though the cigarettes did seem to worsen my headache tenfold. Completely aware of the end result, I never hesitated. There was no denying myself the opportunity for more anesthesia.

I already knew who was calling. No one else would've dared to call me at that hour. They knew better because I only plugged in the phone when I needed to make a call, but lately I hadn't been able to remember to unplug it, oddly enough.

She always called late at night. At first I was pissed, but she was lovely and brilliant – the closest to true love that I would ever get. I knew soon her voice would make me want her, no matter what. Another painfully euphoric addiction, the likes of which I simply could not deprive myself.

"Miles?" she asked, concerned, as if I were sick. It was disheartening to hear her try to sound so worried. This meant that our conversation should be serious. I was in no condition for this. I should have never answered, but something about Lauren, maybe everything about her, made me want to hear her demented heart calling out for me – a hyper-drug of another breed, more addicting and destructive than all the others.

"Hey. What's wrong?" I asked. "Everything all right?"

"Yeah, I'm fine. How have you been?" she asked, giving me a chance to wake before she started.

"Fine," I said. "I've been fine. You?" She answered, but I didn't listen.

I lay back down, propping my head against a pillow. The girl lying next to me, whose name I couldn't remember, wrestled in her sleep then nestled under my arm and laid her head on my chest. We had met earlier at the beach and she was exceptionally beautiful, but her name was not, otherwise I might have remembered it. Maybe a color of some type or a jewel of some fashion: Amber or Jade or Diamond or Violet. I had no fucking idea. When she originally told me her name I could only think of how it could possibly be that something so beautiful was named after something so aloof as a color or a rock. I imagined myself kicking her father's balls through his stomach and face-pushing her mother to the ground, scolding their collective frivolity. The image made me smile just after she had said something cute. Good timing never hurt.

"Where were you tonight? I called earlier but there was no answer." Lauren spoke to me out of concern, but for whom I wasn't sure. I sensed that her intentions were tainted, that she was after something other than my well-being. She was a thousand miles away, and I could still feel her digging, hoping to catch me doing something to her disapproval, giving her more reason for not having me in her life anymore. Maybe she wasn't. Maybe she was just being the quietly amazing girl that I had fallen in love with so long ago.

"I was up near Lake Conroe doing some research so I can finish this fucking article."

My day was actually spent the same as all the others, wading in the salty waters of Wolf Bay drinking beer and smoking dope, pulling in redfish as the sun crept up over the Gulf of Mexico. For some time, Lauren had been under the false impression that I had taken a position with *Texas Fisherman* and was writing under the pen name of Sam Shaw Buckley. It was all bullshit. I'd had a collection of essays and short stories published about two years prior called *Shredded Thoughts of an Animal*. As a result, I received a rather large advance (at least to me) from a publishing house in New York to complete my first novel.

I didn't have time to kill. Time had that advantage. The novel had become a squirming, throbbing slop of a monster. When it crossed my mind the thought disturbed me. Confined me. Cornered me. Trapped me. I wanted to kill it, but they wouldn't let me. After reading the first one hundred pages or so, and with some evil coercing from my agent in Chicago, they decided to take the chance. He was a snake in the grass, my agent. The most obnoxious, conniving Jew you'd ever find and a smile worth every penny you've got. His name was Finkel, and I loved him.

My deadline for the first draft was over three months before, and yet I had written no more than what they had already read. I was still living off the little that remained of my advance. That and the fairly modest royalty checks from *Shredded Thoughts* were just enough to keep me in quality booze and drugs without allowing me to appear to be the strung-out junkie that I really was. It was a matter of pacing myself with the timely influx of money, and it was working perfectly. I just ignored their calls and rejected the certified letters, occasionally dropping a note by mail that things were coming along fine and a bit more time would be needed for some last-minute changes. I felt a lawsuit coming on but not much else.

I slipped my fingers into the shimmering auburn hair that lay across my chest. It smelled of cigarettes and fine perfume, a blend of fresh peaches and blooming honeysuckle beneath a finely spun web of smoke. The hues of cinnamon and scarlet were engaging and the touch was soft and cool and she excited me. I moved my hand down the small of her back and rubbed the warm firmness between her inner thighs. She was a beach junkie from what I could tell. Her tan body was smooth and tight, painted with narrow tan lines from her white g-string swimsuit, which seemed to enhance her already perfect figure. She was absolutely gorgeous. I wasn't sure how we got there. The details dissolved away in a twisted haze of pot, valium, beer, scotch, pain killers and saltwater.

My only definitive memory of the day was seeing a rather large alligator, nine feet or so, leap from the water's muddy tranquility and devour a whooping crane in the shard of a second. Just in front of me the water crashed, shattered by the lashing strength of a brilliant, scaled survivor of eternity. The crane vanished, and the great dragon disappeared. Within seconds the water was calm and quiet, as if nothing had happened. It was both amazing and beautiful, and being that I was standing in the same muddy water some fifteen feet away, it scared the shit out of me, too. What had happened was real, awesome life and in my own sick way I felt damn lucky to have seen it happen.

"I miss you, Miles," Lauren said. "It's been hard being away from you like this." I could hear her voice breaking. She wanted to cry. I wished she wouldn't, but said nothing. "Why is this so difficult? Why can't we just let it go? Why Miles?" This was just too much for me at that point, and I wanted to be sleeping again, but it was Lauren, my Lauren. I couldn't stand the thought of tears in her eyes, and she knew it.

Lauren asked questions for which I had no answers. She knew I didn't have the answers. She just wanted me to know her questions and wondered if mine were the same. Mine were the same. I just never asked them. Not to her. Not to anyone. After all, it was her decision to separate before she left for Spain to spend several months sharpening her already extraordinary painting skills. I fought her hard on this, but she was determined to go away without leaving any ties behind. Ten years being side by side cut loose and left to drift in the cold Chicago wind in case something better lay in waiting overseas. You know, some dude with a scarf and all that stuff. Though it could have been payback for my deserting her in Chicago after we had both worked so hard to build a life there together. "I get no inspiration here," I remember telling her. At least that was my excuse. I believed it anyway, and eventually she did, too. Really it was nothing more than my being homesick, away from the warmth of the coastal waters and my insurgent love for fishing the salty bays cut just inland off the Texas coast. "Everything's frozen here!" I'd screamed. "I'm frozen here!" It all happened so fast. It wasn't until after I'd been gone for several months that she gathered I had chosen the water over her. I had to. Though it wasn't just the water – it was everything that home had always meant to me: the weather, the space, the pace and the people. I had spent my life barefoot in the sands of the Texas coast – before that, I was just a child surrounded by miles and miles of nothing but miles and miles of West Texas desert. I remembered the people there. Real cowboys. They were good and honest and humble. Buried memories: horseback rides, creosote, cattle drives, campfires, unobstructed sunrises and sunsets, absolute silence, stunning solitude. I missed those times, though all the details were unclear. I recalled that it was there, in the midst of all that is natural and real that I first saw God. Tucked away amidst the mesquite and pear flats and the great sky, I felt the presence of something greater and so much more humble than I could ever be surrounding me, loving me fully and without condition. It was the dawn of a day. Horseback with my grandfather. The sky burned and glowed in rich blue and the day broke and let us in. I would never be the same again.

As a result of my time in the bays and desert brush, I had eaten mostly wild game since I could remember. In Chicago I was called a murderer on several occasions by some of Lauren's concrete-footed, air-kissing friends. Krisie, Lauren's friend from school, came to me one night at her own opening at the Art Institute of Chicago and rather nonchalantly called me "a killer" in front of several of the other turtlenecks. This disturbed me.

"It takes a lot of balls to drive through McDonald's."

I killed my beer and left. I'm no critic. I never wanted to be. Those people are too opinionated. They're paid and overpaid for something as silly as their opinions. That's like being paid to fart. Hell, I could've never spent it all.

Lauren stood next to me during the little "killer" exchange, her lips smiling and quiet. I carried that vision of her with me as she stayed behind and I walked down Michigan Avenue smoking a joint in the heavy snow and the hollow sound of distant sirens.

I hopped a train back up to Wrigleyville, built a fire, drained a fifth of gin, blacked out, destroyed our apartment, and passed out naked in the bathtub wrapped snuggly in a wet, vomit-soaked rug.

When Lauren got home, she was certain we had been robbed. Our cozy little apartment had been ransacked. Papers everywhere. The little makeshift furniture we had was flipped and broken. Books tossed from the shelves. The phone was ripped off the wall. The ice box doors left open, as was the back door that led down to the alley. I was surprised that I hadn't shit my pants, but Lauren swore no. I never saw the evidence.

Lauren bathed me and carried me to bed with cold water and cool soft sheets. I slept for two days, ate soup and drank water and wine and tried to remember what had happened. After Lauren brought home a new phone cord, I came to discover some of what had "transgressed" from Grady O., an old coonass friend in New Orleans. Locally he went by O'Grady. He said that's what the ladies would scream out the second-floor windows in the French Quarter when he was busy poking holes. He said those pretty voices had soon rolled down the Mississippi and snuck into the subconscious of all the other drunks and whores. He was O'Grady then. I called him Grady O.

"You cawled me jus affa midnigh. We tawlkt four bout twenty minutes a so. And YOU tell me you can't never know what is at *I* says, but aftawhile, Mias Jax, I couyldn know shit from your foul mowf, den bam! Line dead."

"Did you try calling me back?"

"You da one called me, muthafucka! Sides, I figures yous dead inihows."

"That's thoughtful, but I'm not dead."

"Not yet you ain't fish man." He laughed, and I could hear him fighting back the brown mucus in his throat and lungs. "I gotta go, Mias Jax. Water's a callin."

He hung up. He went. Still going. I missed that crazy bastard. He was a good one, Grady O. We'd met in Louisiana on a back swamp fishing trip several years before. Grady O. was the sweet swamp creature. He drank more than anyone I had ever met. Ever. Laughed hard at your jokes and twice as hard at his own. His laugh was a spew of spit, a billowing hiss of tar-clogged air leaking out under enormous pressure, exploding into a halitonic fireball of charming, infected, infectious laughter. Grady O. was shameless when it came to the use of the malapropism. The first night by the fire, he blurted out such verbal fineries as "if one you boys drowned, can't nobody hold me reliable for shit!" and "for all intensive purposes he would not be objective to drowning to death" and "when the rainy season come along, it come along one shit-sized sheet of participation afta anotha." On our first night of the trip Grady O. told me that he could tell just by looking at me that I "had an infinity toward animals."

"You think so, Grady O.?"

"I know so, Mias Jax."

"That's nice of you to say."

One moist morning, Grady O. and I were fishing together deep in the swamp. We were drunk and freshly stoned from some fine red-haired bud I'd been saving. Suddenly, he announced that he was "one hongry hardass" and took the last piece of jerky from my shirt pocket, stuffing it into his toothless mouth. I stared at him as he moaned and smiled, gumming the last of the food on board.

"I suspect, vaginally, of course, that you know it's only right to share, Grady O."

"Far unuff." He slopped and smacked and reached his dirty sausage fingers into his mouth, somehow managing to gnaw the saliva-soaked swirl of jerky in two. He held out a piece and placed into my hand. I stuffed it into my mouth and chewed and moaned with great delight – then swallowed. Grady O. vomited his sloppy portion overboard.

"That a way to chum it up." I said. "We'll be catching em by the net fulls now."

9

After a few seconds had passed, he said that he regretted throwing-up and that now he was hungrier than before. I immediately spoke of the likes of shrimp etouffee, hot crawfish gumbo and boudin with wild rice and red beans. He asked me to stop, and I did. Then I started again. "What do you cook best, Grady O.?" We got to talking about cooking. He said muffins were his favorite thing to cook. His mama had taught him how using wild blackberries, fresh peaches, jalapeno peppers and goat cheese. I told him that the smell of jalapenos reminded me of West Texas. The smells of my grandfather's cattle ranch in the foothills of the Chinati Mountains along the Rio Grande. I told him how it all seemed like a myth to me. A place that was too real and too safe, and the times too short and too happy. They seemed more like fantasies than vague memories. I told Grady O. that I was curious as to why I only had good memories from that place. They were few, but they were good. All few of them. They weren't like the few other childhood memories I had. My first fight. My first kiss. My first beating. My last beating. I bled my stoned heart out to Grady O. on that boat, and he slept through every fucking word. I woke him by slapping his face with a twenty-six-inch trout. I slapped the piss out of him. He awoke farting and coughing out something about how "one ought to be mighty careful in them Wess Texas mountains cause ovens cook diffirent at higher evaluations. The dough raises slower at sea level. But you know what, Mias Jax? The sea don't stay level for long. You think too hard on it, and it ain't level no wheres. Take me back to camp muthafucka, I'm hungry like hell."

I took him to camp, and we both passed out in old Adirondack chairs with fish in our mouths, cloaked in blankets of mosquitoes, a slight lift of smoke from that morning's breakfast fire filtering up into the magnificently mossed trees.

When I woke to leave, Grady O. was already gone. Fishing somewhere. He left his business card curled-up in my left nostril. It read *O'Grady Deautrive*. There was a handwritten phone number and grease marks on the card. That was it. Grady O. and I made good friends on that trip.

I was unaware at the time, but that would be my last conversation with Grady O. I didn't know why I'd called Grady O. that night. I never knew what my motivations were while I was in blackout, but the more I thought about it the more I understood the importance of empathy and understanding. The freedom given by the utter lack of judgment. Seeking counsel from one who would smile through what would have easily killed me. That's all it was.

When Lauren got home the following evening, we laughed about what had happened at the art opening, and then she laughed some more. I loved her so much for being righteous that night.

It did hurt me to leave Lauren. I'll never forget the salty taste of her tears as we kissed goodbye. I hoped that she would come with me, but she couldn't. Her life was in Chicago, and she was flourishing there, but I was only happy there when I was with her. These times were just too infrequent, and, when we weren't together I was no different from the leafless maples that lined the corner of Racine and West Addison. Cold. Still. Unseen.

"Have you been seeing anyone?" For this question, she did expect an answer. Fuck her for asking. Knowing she was anxious, I waited to offer my response. Her audacity angered me, and it was none of her business anymore. She'd have to wait. That was part of this stupid fucking game, and it was punishment for prying into my life after throwing me away without a thought. "Miles, have you?"

"No," I lied. But sinners sin. I closed my eyes, my head throbbed and spun. My stomach swam with hot nausea, and I held back a strong urge to vomit. Maybe I was just feeling guilty, but guilty of what? I had done nothing. If she loved me, she'd have known that was true. Giving love, true love, is granting unconditional freedom and then living in a complete state of faith. If she had understood this, I wouldn't have had to wade through all that conciliatory bullshit.

"Do you miss me, Miles?" she asked. "Do you ever think about me anymore, MyJax?" She was strategic with her questions. They were loaded in one way or another. Either I could answer to her liking and she would be happy or satisfied or whatever she felt when I showed her no opposition, or I could play hard and lie to her and say that I didn't miss her anymore and that I went days without the thought of her. Then she would curse me and my name and my pathetic life of drunken emptiness and the line would go dead. This was no time to argue. I tried to speak as little as possible, but she called me MyJax like she used to when we were together and happy.

"Of course," I said quietly, trying to answer without making the girl next to me suspicious. Not that it mattered – I didn't even know her name nor did I really care for her being next to me anymore. Though she did feel much cleaner than the regular girls at The Surfside down by the canal overpass.

"You do what, Miles?" Lauren asked, forcing it out of me.

"Miss you." The auburn-haired girl didn't move, and Lauren seemed to accept my weak response without suspicion. I wanted to hang up now and sleep and forget about my life for a while. "I've got to sleep now. I have a deadline to meet tomorrow, and I'm exhausted."

She said okay and that she would let me rest. She was sorrowful and lovely. I wanted to hold her and make love to her again. She would tell me she loved me always and that she was mine. And we'd sleep and love into daybreak until sunlight or work or something of the unfair world forced us to break away from one another. Then the emptiness would come and grow heavier each time.

The line went dead, and I gently reached over the auburn-haired girl and hung up. Lying back down, she looked up at me. "Someone important, Miles?" she asked, smiling a syrupy, chalk-white smile. Her face sculptured in sharp, clean angles. Just the sight of her overwhelmed me with the urge to fuck. My aches and nausea vanished, and all I wanted to do was fuck this beautiful woman. She was just one of those few whose beauty sang to me. Crimson-colored lips, plump and portly, my god, then her name, her parents. What the fuck were these simpletons thinking? It was something similar to a stage name for a topless dancer or a cute nickname from childhood, but she wasn't joking nor did it seem to bother her. Understandably so – beauty in such great proportions overshadows any name, even Cranston. Cranston? I had friends who named their second daughter Cranston. I didn't even know what that meant, and I refused to speak the name/word aloud because doing so brought to mind the look and smell of heavily soiled carpet padding. I didn't dare to categorize this murky stew of vowels and consonants a name, much less a meaningful word in any language, ebonics included. I heard that it might be the name of some town outside Pittsburgh, but I couldn't bring myself to do the research. Had I seen this condemned, jagged string of letters on a map, I feared I might have raged uncontrollably and shit myself. Then I'd have been forced to wander about, unsure if I had ever met or seen anyone from Cranston, Pennsylvania. A Cranstonite. A Cranstonian. Cranstonoids. The night after my friends bequeathed to their newborn the aforementioned "C-name/word" as a name, I slept rather restlessly due to the trauma of maintaining my silence. I so desperately wanted them to take it back, to sleep on it, to try again, try harder. The name/word seared itself into my mind, and I dreamed that there was a thirteenth apostle named Cranston. Jesus asked him to go out and bring back to him the Son of God. Cranston took off with great fervor, but never came back, and they all chuckled and joked about it at the Last Supper.

"No one important, gal," I lied. It didn't matter. It wasn't important what she knew, and I wasn't going to waste my time worrying about it. Worry is a choice and such a wasteful burden.

We kissed, and she laid her head on my chest, stroking my stomach with her thin hands and long, clear fingernails. She moved her hands beneath the sheets and rubbed her fingers through my pubic hair then massaged and stroked me. I had forgotten about being sick, about being behind in the world outside, about not writing at all and drinking and drugging. I wanted this beautiful stranger next to me and soon I was in her, and we danced and swayed like thick, warm fluid. She was lovely and soft and perfect. Her movement was strong and commanding, and her sweat felt good on me.

When we finished, I lay on top of her, and she lightly rubbed my back as our breathing relaxed. We said nothing, and I did not look at her. It was warm in my room, but I was cold and wet with sweat and began to get dizzy again. When I closed my eyes it only worsened. I pulled out of her quickly – she gasped and smiled as though unexpectedly being splashed with cold water. I moved to the edge of the bed and sat up trying to fight off the twirling room, the taste of blood and bile and rotten flesh. Slowly standing, I made my way toward the bathroom. I could feel her eyes on me as I stumbled away, nauseous and cooked from the sun and drugs and booze.

"You all right, Miles?" she asked, genuinely concerned. "You gonna be okay? Can I do anything for you, sweetheart?"

"Yeah, leave."

"What?"

"It'd be wise of you to leave now and never come back. You're a very beautiful woman, and I enjoyed loving you."

I shut the bathroom door behind me and locked it. I fell to my knees, cold sweat beaded on my back, and I heaved and vomited in the darkness. The growing smell of necrotic tissue stung deep in my sinuses. I spat bloody bits and bile slime into the commode trying to catch my breath. I was glad not to see it as I flushed it away and lay down on the cold tile floor embracing a dubious sense of relief, unsure if I would vomit again. Hoping once was enough, I prayed for the same. It seemed to be the only time I remembered myself asking anyone for help. That was just something I would never do again. It wasn't worth it.

Grabbing a towel off the floor, I covered myself. The towel was still damp from my shower earlier, but it was soft and heavy and felt like the arms of my mother. I closed my eyes and tried to sleep, to be still, to rest before I tried again. I vomited a string of mucus that would not break nor relent until it was expelled from my body. After an exhausting fight for air and peace, I lay back on the cold floor exhausted and spent. I heard my name called by a child and soon fell into the sleep that had been evading me for too long.

date

Evil has the consistency of water. It somehow finds its way into the most unexpected places. A wolf in sheep's clothing. A sinner beneath a saintly robe. An obvious bore in the scream of excitement.

Suzanne was what I considered normal. I found that interesting. Her shoulder-length hair was sandy blonde with large rolling curls. It was natural and innocent, but when the wind blew her hair across her blue eyes, she was sexy and small and exotic. She was not the type of girl to whom I previously had been drawn. Suzanne was educated and articulate, and, when she spoke, I thought of Hemingway. I told her this, but she had no response – as if I had told her nothing new.

After dinner, we drove to the beach and drank more wine and listened to the waves crash the shore. I let down the windshield of my old Jeep, and we held hands and kissed. The wind blew wildly, and her hair splashed in all directions – but she was certain of herself, and it didn't bother her. I respected that about Suzanne. It was extraordinary to be with someone who was stable and simple and caring in a traditional way, the way I remember my family sometimes being. Holiday families. She came right off the beaten path, that is to say she came straight from mid-stream America, from a sound family, content with who she was and what life would bring her. In an odd way, this made me want to be with her and listen to the strange things she said. They were so different from anything I had ever wanted to hear. They were simple and common, boring to the point of fascination. She was my window to all the things common and real and sober, things that had been occurring outside the reckless succession of mishaps and chaos that had become my life. Everything about her was laced with a calming streak of normalcy. She had the faith. Blind faith. Faith by The Book. I could never grasp this orthodoxy. Doing so was conforming and conformity was for the masses and the herds and the inmates and the dead.

Suzanne was content with a good job. I always believed there was nothing good about any job.

"I like it here, Miles," she said. "The salt air is so nice. Nothing else smells quite like it." It was nice, and the summer wind was warm and soothing. "You like the salt water, don't you, Miles?"

"Yeah, I guess I do," I said. "I like it very much. I lived not too far from here when I was a child."

I loved the salt water because it had always been a part of my life, and I knew that living by it and being in it throughout my childhood somehow made me different from other people who never had the opportunity to experience life on the bay. I wanted to tell her all about life on the water's edge and give her insight into its mystery and beauty and danger. I wanted her to know how I used to fish in the mornings with my grandmother and how she taught me to spit on the bait if the fish weren't biting. And how my mother grew aloe plants in the yard so the healing fluids inside would always be nearby when I came home red and burning from the biting tentacles of the jellyfish.

I hoped Suzanne wouldn't want to swim. It was only a few days prior since I last swam at that beach. It was with a girl I'd met at a blues bar on The Strand, and she was fat and unattractive and loud, but I was drunk, and we swam naked in the dark surf and had sex on the shore among the seaweed and dying cabbage heads.

She'd asked if I would drive her through Jack-in-the-Box on the way home. I did it without a word, but with complete admiration for her having the audacity or stupidity or ignorance even to ask. Ice water for me, the rest of the menu and the rest of my money for her. At her apartment complex, we exchanged numbers. She gave me hers, and I gave her the number to Pizza Hut. I figured she might as well call someone who would answer. Poor gal.

"Sometimes I want to burst with curiosity when I think of your life, Suzanne. It's like looking for the mountains where there's nothing but endless, flat plains. It's amazing."

"I don't understand what you mean."

"I don't either, really. I just enjoy examining the life you live. It's queerly interesting."

"Queerly interesting?"

"Absolutely. It's like watching gay people live their lives. It's so close to my own yet it's too difficult for me to understand, much less participate in. You just wonder what goes through the minds of these folks."

"What are you saying? Do you think I'm gay?"

"No. I'm saying that being with you is similar to being with a homo. It's different and interesting and strange. You can just think of the other person as a human being and observe him in that way since there's no way on God's great earth any fucking's gonna take place."

She took her hand away from me, and I looked at her. She wasn't smiling anymore, and her big blue eyes seemed troubled. She sat on her hands as if to warm them.

"You scare me, Miles."

"What have I done to scare you?"

"Nothing, Miles. You do nothing. That scares the hell out of me. Not to mention that you just told me that you think I'm gay – I think. I don't want to hurt you, but you're childish, and your thoughts seem so dangerous. And what about the way you live, Miles? The way you roam around without any particular destination? There's no settlement in you. You just want to fish and drink all the time and you don't care what lies ahead. It's a cop-out, Miles. I'm so sorry to say this to you, but it's the way I feel."

She seemed scared. "Is it responsibility that scares you, Miles?"

"I've reason to feel no fear of anything or anyone. Never again. Ever."

I tried to find the best way to say it.

"Life and death have fallen off the scales. I've always known about it, but I never let myself receive it. Then, I finally did."

"That's exactly what I mean, Miles. You're speaking drunken nonsense. Are you scared of failing? You say you're a writer, but I've never seen anything that you've written."

"It wouldn't be in your section."

"That was rude."

"I didn't mean it that way. I just meant it's probably not next to the breath mints and batteries."

"All I've ever seen you do is scribble on napkins and fish and drink. At night, you disappear, then call and wake me as if I want to hear you slur and snore. It frightens me because I don't know you well enough, but you don't seem to care. It's as though we've been dating for years, Miles. It's just too strange for me. I need stability in my life, and you have none, none for yourself much less any for me. I'm sorry, Miles, and I know this sounds hateful, but we've been very honest with one another so far. I think that's the best way."

I wanted her to stop talking. The urge to grab her by the face and squeeze her mouth shut passed through my syrupy thoughts, but I was a drunk and a drug addict, not a woman beater. I never had a cell of sympathy for those chickenshits. Life is unfair, but to punish a woman because of it is outright cowardice. Besides, she was right. She did deserve someone better than me, and I knew that particular someone would not be difficult to find: a banker, an insurance salesman, a real estate broker or maybe a drug store manager, someone with a job and short-sleeve shirt and a dirty little tie, someone with some self-respect, someone who listened growing up, someone blind to the thrills and ills of my side of life.

We rolled down the Sea Wall. She was crying now. She didn't want to hurt me, but she thought she had, and it made her sad because being sweet was her nature. But she hadn't hurt me. You can't kill a dead man. I was already there. I just had to abide by the notion.

"Take me home please, Miles."

I did so without speaking another word to her. Even when she said goodbye and walked away, I said nothing. As I drove away, I thought of how lovely she was at the beach with her hair dancing in the wind. I stopped and wrote the words *splashing hair* on the top of my hand, then continued on. I would never see nor speak with Suzanne again.

home

Around four in the morning I arrived home from a five hundred dollar night at Surfside Cabaret. I had taken the liberty of drowning out a typical evening with a bottle of scotch and two dancers in the dressing room behind the club. One of them was missing her two front teeth.

"You might want to quit gnawing so hard on the headboard back at the trailer."

That bought me a slap on the face and new pair of aching blue balls for the ride home. I think the other one had most of her teeth, but when she sided with her friend and decided she didn't need my shit either, I lied to her and told her she had a case of halitosis that'd make your socks roll up and down. They called me a brat and an asshole and a drunk, but somehow, Pop, the owner and my good friend, my source to let me be, let it pass. He poured me into the Jeep and sent me on my way. Life in a small town is so big sometimes.

Orange lightning split across a dark blue sky as my bare feet sank into the dew-soaked Saint Augustine. I stumbled to the old wooden landing at the base of the stairs that led up to my apartment above the garage. Abilene, my landlord's German Shepherd and my dear, dear friend, came to me and licked the sweat from my face with all her love. She lay down next to me as the storm moved in off the Gulf. I swallowed greedily from my scotch bottle as though it were warm ranch honey from my childhood. I wanted more. I wanted to be drunker. Pushing the sweat on my forehead back into my hair, I spat strongly into the grass and watched to see where it landed. The night was churning with angry thunderheads, and I was in it – full of booze and empty of heart.

I stood and stepped into the grass and urinated in the yard, swaying in the wind but not because of it. Abilene watched anxiously from beneath a wooden bench waiting for me to finish so that she could investigate. She did so as I tediously sat back down and drank some more. The great live oaks swayed in the wind, and the rain finally began to fall. It felt like the beginning of a pretty song.

I let the rain fall on me until I was completely soaked. I took off my shirt and dropped it next to me. Abby sniffed at it, then moved upstairs, closer to the front door, trying to get out of the rain. I let the rain drench me with its nourishment. The neighbors hated me anyway. I bathed in the cold rain shower. It was lovely.

The storm howled and screamed. I drank hard from the bottle again and, in a bright flash, I saw the words *splashing hair* draining down my hand. I finished undressing until I was completely naked. It felt good being naked. I was vulnerable and unprotected, and it was nice to be fearless and completely exposed. Once more, I pissed in the yard – this time from the top step, swaying back and forth as if blindfolded on the cliff's edge.

Stepping toward the front door, I knocked over the whiskey bottle. It clunked boringly down the wet steps and bled into the soupy soil.

Falling into my bed, I found it still messy and dirty from the night before. The old Indian blanket my grandmother made was soft beneath me, and I rolled on it trying to dry myself. In the still darkness of my apartment, sweet old Abilene slept beside me.

morning

The noise grew disturbingly louder as I came to. It was the persistent honking of a squeaking foreign horn. It came from the car of my childhood friend and landlord, Louie. Louie was the proud owner of Louie's Waterfront Café, a fine-dining establishment built on a grand pier over the bay's edge in a booming area of town called Anglers Pointe which is composed mainly of large, newly built homes with rolling bay windows and large wrap-around decks. The only permanent residents there were a few retired folks who had spent their lives in dark suits scraping their leather-soled shoes across the concrete of the big city sidewalks, amassing fortunes in order to come to a place like this and brown their wrinkled skin as they adjust their hearing aids to the great silence of the still waters. The rest of the houses stayed empty most of the time, except for holidays and weekends, when the others rushed in like a white squall, carting in their fancy fishing gear and loaded wallets.

I could already picture him in my mind, dressed in his standard morning costume: a white short sleeve button-down, pleated khaki shorts, both Polo, of course, and both starched to the inflexible feel of double-walled cardboard, a mahogany colored alligator skin belt and maroon penny loafers – no socks, with pennies. It surprised me that he didn't get his ass kicked on a daily basis, but I finally realized this was due to his superb ass-kissing ability. Most folks might think he was some sort of blue bleeding vagina, but not me. I knew Louie. I grew up with him. He always worked, and he always worked harder than anyone I knew.

I stepped naked down the stairs. I saw that expression of anger on his puffy olive-flavored face just as I had imagined. If it weren't for all the honking, I would have slipped into some shorts, but Louie couldn't stand embarrassment, and I couldn't stand loud annoying noises.

"Don't come out here like that, asshole!" he barked from behind the open door of his shiny black Range Rover.

"Just knock, Lou-Lou. There's no need to go wakin up the whole neighborhood."

"They're awake. It's Wednesday."

As my feet hit the concrete surface of the driveway, Louie took a guarded position with one loafer on the ground, the other on the floorboard of the Range Rover, just in case I suddenly came at him with my looming morning trunk. We had been friends since the age of seven, and, when we hit puberty, my dick outgrew my body and his just drifted off to the left. It was a strange phenomenon within our circle of friends how my cock had over-matured, and theirs just got hairy and remained childishly dormant.

"Where's that bitch? She needs to move that piece of shit." Louie pointed to the deep purple Honda Accord parked behind him.

Celeste was so proud of her new car. It was three years old, but to her it was new and to me it was better than walking. Personally, I would have selected another color, as it did resemble a profound extraterrestrial bruise on wheels. Louie loved to hate that car. It was his way of releasing jealous steam over my having a promiscuous relationship with his barkeep. He begged me to stay away from her, but never gave a reason, so I correctly assumed jealousy and steadfastly ignored his request.

At the edge of the driveway, I pissed in the grass. "Give her a minute, Lou-Lou. She's coming."

"Are you proud of yourself?"

"I'm not expecting a fucking trophy."

While I was steadily draining my bulging bladder, Celeste descended the stairs toward me wearing her faded blue jeans and one of my weathered t-shirts and holding her wrinkled work clothes in the curl of one arm and her shoes and purse in the other. Her long, black curly hair blew in the breeze, brushing across the brilliant blue of her feline-spotted eyes. Those eyes were like fire, and I melted into them. She was twenty-three, ferociously beautiful and free-spirited with a heart hardened from a life of poverty and abuse, but somewhere, for some reason, in that jagged heart was a soft spot for me.

"You need to be ready by ten o'clock," Louie snapped at Celeste.

She kissed me on the lips and patted my rear, "Bye, sugar." Mutually distasteful glares ensued as she passed Louie.

"Don't be late."

"I'll be there."

"You'd better."

"Fuck you."

And my beautiful angel slipped away in a revolting strip of deep purple.

Louie stood there giving me his usual vermicular expression of disappointment, shaking his head and sighing, his Rolex glimmering in the sunshine. It was so hard to take him seriously. Or maybe it was just easier not to take him seriously.

"It hasn't even been ninety days yet."

"Actually it's been ninety-three days and ninety-three nights."

25

"Well, shit, I guess that's enough time to get over true love. You're such a bullshitter. You've never loved anyone in your life, have you, Miles?"

As I approached Louie, he shuddered as if to be ready to make a sudden escape. "That's just it, Lou-Lou. If love is true, it's never over."

"Yeah. Did you tell that to Lauren?"

"Who do you love, Louie?" I asked, getting closer.

"How about putting some clothes on and getting some writing done? I'm going broke over here."

"Who do you love, Louie?"

"I'm not kidding, asshole. How long until you're done? I'm tired of Barbara on my ass, and I'd like to rent this place to someone who actually pays."

"Inspiration, baby, inspiration." I went at him with open arms.

"Goddammit! Don't do that shit out here!" he screeched, jumping in the Rover and slamming the door behind him.

I rubbed my oily face hard against his window. "You know you love me. Show me you love me, Louie. Come on, just show me."

"Get some work done, you sorry bastard!" He sped backward into the street, just missing my toes. I chased after him in an over-exaggerated trot, black-and-white slow motion. He sped away with the flip of his finger shadowed by my greasy facial imprint, leaving me alone at the street's edge. He was headed straight for the carwash. I would've bet my short-ass life on it. Some things, well, just people really, never change.

Louie was right about it being Wednesday. The entire street was abandoned and silent. Everyone was gone. I gazed about and engulfed the silence as if there were a whisper waiting to be heard. The sunlight danced on my skin through the sea-blown oak trees swaying in the breeze. As I began to make my way back to my apartment, I wondered why it was that Wednesday was not pronounced the way it was actually spelled. This thought captured me, and in my mind, I saw weddings and white dresses, music and dance, and I was there drinking and watching the formal garments toss in the wind and song.

It was a deep voice and a blotch of pale blue in the corner of my eye that made the music stop. Darla, our kind mail carrier, stood frozen next to the step of Louie's front door. She was pale white and obese, her cheeks red with exhaustion. "How boutcha, Darla?"

"Miles, you're naked," she said, almost motherly.

"I was born this way." With two quick steps, I snatched the mail from the firm clench of her swollen hand. "I'll take that." Walking away, I sorted through the stash. "Be good now, Darla."

"I ain't sure that's legal, Miles," Darla shouted as I rounded the side of the house.

"You too, gal."

It was my royalty check from *Shredded Thoughts* that I was after. It was about that time, and I needed the money. The drugs and booze were beginning to grow scarce. And there it was. The elegant lettering engraved on the envelope gave it away every month.

I deposited Louie's portion of the mail at his back doorstep. The day was enormous, and I could feel an evening of fishing menacing in my blood. Ripping open my mail, I quickly made my way back to the stairs that led to my apartment. My feet hitting the steps, I could feel Barbara's eyes upon me from the second story of the main house – she always kept a watchful eye, despising me the way she did. Not by accident, I dropped my check and had to bend deeply over in order to retrieve it. Whether she enjoyed this or not, I knew I did. Get a fucking job or mind your own business or both.

After setting my alarm for three that afternoon, I smoked a bowl, ate a slice of orange, drank warm water from an open plastic bottle then crashed like thunder and dreamt like rain.

afternoon

The valiums in my belly were dissolving nicely as the ice-cold beer flowed in. It was around three-thirty when I arrived at the marina, and the water was a gorgeous emerald green, beckoning me like a call from some home. From the back of the Jeep I grabbed Old Faithful, my rod and reel, and the wading belt that I had made equipped with a floating, waterproof tackle box. This belt was one of my few proud possessions, outfitted with a holder for Old Faithful hand-carved from driftwood, a stringer with a bright red corked end, a detachable floating koozie and a healthy plethora of zipped pockets loaded with a large flask of scotch, top-water jigs, rubber worms of all colors, leads and treble hooks, needle-nose pliers, a roll of twelve-pound line, three beers on ice, my collapsible, magnetized stainless steel pipe that I'd bought in New York City, and a variety of prescription medications – non-prescribed, of course. My belt, to me, was an invention of perfection. When it was locked on, I was hands-free and ready to fish, but never too far from any necessity. After thirty-two years on the planet, that was my most, my only, commendable accomplishment. Thank you.

After the valium had dissolved its way into my bloodstream, several heavy handed pain killers with my beer was a nice follow-up. Lately, too much at once had begun to make me vomit – which I could only attribute to not eating enough – so I began to watch the timing of my dosages. What was the point of rearranging reality if you didn't feel so good?

I could see Piggy readying the nets as Pop's boat, Freeloader (named after me he often claimed), made its way out into the channel. It was about a fifty-yard trot from the pavement to the pier to the bow of the boat. I leapt aboard and set down my gear. It felt as though I had run a thousand miles dragging a hundred pound bag of shit, but it didn't matter. I was on my way, and the day was stunning, and the salt stirred in my veins, and black-spotted tails flapped and splashed at the banks of my soul.

"How boutcha boys?" I asked. They both smiled, still tending to their business. They were used to my standard greeting, but I was in the habit of saying it because it had always intrigued me as to what kind of response I would get, especially not knowing myself if what I was saying was a question or a statement or what. It was something I remember my grandfather saying when I was child. He had spent all his life cattle ranching in Far West Texas. I recalled him as a rough cowboy and a kind man. I figured since it was okay for him, it was fine for me, too. He died before we ever had a chance to live lives as two men seated in cottonwood shade while our horses watered at the spring. I imagined how it might have been, how it would have changed me or made me different, but it was just wonder, and that's all it ever would be.

As I got older, I realized my grandfather's greeting could tell me volumes about a person, depending on their particular response. The first time I met Pop, a soft-spoken, hard-weathered shrimper of forty-five years at sea, he just smiled at me when I how bouted him – not a tooth in sight, nor an ounce of shame for it, much less anything else. He was salt of the earth and did, in time, become my good friend – my earthly father. Piggy, the only black man in town and Pop's deckhand for over twenty years, just responded with a simple "Awrl-rite-den." I liked it because it was just as confusing as "how boutcha?" It made me feel that somewhere in the opposite color of our fabric was a common thread that wove a bond of friendship between us.

"I feel Mud Cut today, Pop. I mean I'm feeling the fuck outta this one."

"You feel it, do ya?"

"Yezzir, I do. I do indeed."

"He feels it again, Pig."

"Look out," Piggy smiled. "Miles done got that damned ole feelin again."

With my feet dragging in the cool water, I took a half a joint from my shirt pocket and lit it. Neither Pop nor Piggy ever gave me any hassle about it, and neither partook, though I had offered many times. They made their living working with Mother Nature, and as Pop once told me, "After so many years of life on the sea you learn to just let things be as they're supposed to."

Once, I asked him about his cabaret down by the overpass.

"Gotta make a livin."

And I understood him as he stood hard and humble next to me and sailed us across the quiet waters. I admired both the men. They were old and strong, gentle and determined, quiet and content. Looking back at them working that old boat, I realized it was just simple second nature swirled in a pure salty passion. Smiling with great comfort as we hit the channel, I was feeling warm and ready.

"Can't fight the feelin," I whispered, and out into the bay we sailed.

In order to keep from stirring up the water, Pop slowed Freeloader to a slight chug as we entered Mud Cut. It was a courtesy to me, and I appreciated his kindness. I could feel that, in his younger years, he, too, wanted to fish every day, fish for love, not money. Whether or not he approved of the way I lived my life, he appreciated the reality stir of seeing through the saltwater with heart and hand. Joy is there for the taking. He would never deny me that, and he never did.

Mud Cut was not designed for boats the size of Freeloader, nor was it the quickest path to the Gulf of Mexico, but it did lead to "a wealthier piece of water" as Pop called it. This eased my feelings of selfish guilt for being the cause of blowing their sails off course, but I knew by the look of ease and harmony in their eyes that both Pop and Piggy understood, and both would be rewarded handsomely.

Mud Cut was about thirty yards in width at high tide and only about twenty feet deep in the center. The edges of the cut were scattered with the remnants of old fishing camps that had either been wiped out by hurricanes or simply left to rot by owners now dead and gone. These old camps were only accessible by boat. There were no roads to Mud Cut, only roads to places far from the Cut. From there, it was a hike through several miles of swampland that was home to alligators, feral hogs, cottonmouths, seagulls, cranes, pelicans and well-hidden shell pits left behind from the old military artillery training days.

Over the years, I had discovered only one water route to the Cut, and it was only traversable by canoe or kayak. I had kayaked to the Cut many times, but the time came when I no longer had the strength to make it. One of those times that forces you to realize you can no longer do something, that that thing which has been natural to you forever is now gone from you forever. A poor soul and genius of music composition falling deaf at his peak. It scratched at my mind, but I decided not to itch – ever. So catching a ride with Pop and Pig was a great blessing. And so it was, my kayak retired behind Louie's garage, my private route through watery trails of sea grass losing its winding tentacles in the fog of my mind's evaporation and my body's decay.

Bloodshot and concealed by the tint of my sunglasses, my eyes worked the shoreline for the perfect spot. I was looking for anything that might be moving along the banks. If nothing was moving, then I looked for a place where I thought movement might occur as midday gave way to evening. When I found it, I knew it because I could feel it finding me. It was a voiceless breath through my heart singing *yes*.

I nodded at Pop. He cut his engines. I shed my shirt and glasses. The silence was singing on the tips of a gentle breeze. And as though slipping into a pair of torn and faded blue jeans, I slid into the cool water and let my feet sink into the sucking black mud. As the warm top water filled the pits of my arms, I held on to one of the old tires that adorned the sides of Freeloader and submerged my head beneath the surface. This had become my ritual, staying under as long as I could, feeling the thick salt slush fill my ear canals. Eventually my feet were pulled from the mud by the force of the drifting vessel dragging me alongside.

Rising up, I gasped for air and shook the water from my ears. The welcome sight of Piggy's smiling face leaning overboard dissolved away the pungent burn of salt in my eyes. "Forty-two seconds, Mr. Jax," Piggy said, as he handed down my gear. "You must be gettin old on us."

"No sir, it's the smoking catchin up with me. Everything always does."

"Arwl-rite-den! Awrl-rite-den! Pop and I could use a filet or two. We gettin a little tired of eatin bait." He looked back at Pop. "What do ya say, Poppy?"

Pop said nothing. From my position, I couldn't see him, but I knew he agreed.

"Four on the half shell. We'll find out about that ask and receive business, won't we Pig?"

"Yessir we will. We certainly will, Mr. Jax."

I let loose of the tire as Pop fired up the diesels and out into the big, beautiful Gulf of Mexico they glided.

With mud like quicksand after my feet, I shuffled closer to the edge of the Cut. At thigh-deep water, I pulled a cold beer from my belt, took several heavy swallows then set the can in its pouch. Looking at its simple construction of foam, camouflage nylon and velcro, I loved that thing as much as a thing could be loved. I checked the watermelon-colored jig on the end of my line, then spat on it for good luck. It never failed. Every time I spat on bait, live or artificial, visions of my grandmother and me fishing off the pier at our family's old house in Galveston rose in my mind. It was a stucco house on stilts and sat on a large grassy lot out on 6 1/2 Mile Road. Behind the house were picnic benches, an outdoor cold-water shower and a pier jetting about forty paces into the canal. From the road, the house was an exact replica of the Alamo. We called the place Poopy Doo. I didn't know why, and anyone that did was dead. I supposed it didn't really matter. Poopy Doo was gone, wiped out by a raging hurricane. But like the little gusts that remain twirling about that lot, so too do turn certain memories I'll never lose. One of those was MeeMaw telling me to spit on the shrimp before I dropped the line from my little cane pole into the crawling brown water. "Spit on your bait, boy," she said. And I did as I whispered "Tails... tails... tails..." from the silence of Mud Cut, casting Old Faithful at the banks. Life was upon me, and I danced in its cloth, the sun working its needlepoint, the water's current pulling through me and those gorgeous spotted tails making their way to the zip, wind and splash of my watermelon falls.

evening

Pop and Piggy must've had a good run. This was my only thought as I vomited in the tall sea grass. Darkness had led me to shore to dry my skin and rest my aching bones. The evening breeze had died with the sunlight and the raging mosquitoes of the humid Texas coast burst to life with a fury. Without the grass to brush against I'd have had no protection from them. Those fuckers are ruthless as hell fire. It's always blood, blood, blood.

When the grass finally lost its salvation capacity, I resorted to covering my sun-burned skin with the thick mud of the Cut. It dried quickly and was an immense help, but nothing was an end all, so I lay on my back in the grass awaiting the sound of approaching diesel engines, swigging scotch from the flask and swallowing pills that made the mosquito bites feel not too far from the first prick and drip of a dirty heroin needle.

The silence was so immense I wanted to drift to sleep, but the stars were at my fingertips and so many would lose their grip on the world's ceiling and fall away, burning in a shot of white fire through the sky, vanishing forever. I saw one star drop from its still position and ride a fall that seemed cushioned by its close proximity to earth. It was as though the celestial glue which had held it in place since time began finally froze in the arctic emptiness of space and let loose its grip, the great ball of nuclear fusion parachuting to its death.

"I'll remember you."

Now close my eyes. Relax the deteriorated muscles in my body. Find the stillness. Ease the nausea. Absorb the absolute effect of the drugs. Don't get cheated.

By this time, I had to fight to retrieve each slur of the high. Everything was there, but so was my growing tolerance, so I taught myself to slip deeper into my bloodstream and ignite the chemicals I had put there. Reality is best when you don't have to live in it.

Dig in. Find that warm feeling. Like the black mud below the water, the drug resin lay heavy on the bottom of my veins. Relax and bring it to the top. Feel it crawl into my brain and roll back my eyes. Let my teeth gently sear, sending my heart to sleep and my mind to carry on with thoughts of what would be different and when?

Time was of no consequence. It did not exist here. Nothing here existed unless I invited it. It was living invisibly over my imagination. A corpse so deep in death that life itself was nothing but a dream of good things, smiles, life, love and truth. I saw no evil here. I felt only warmth and the tingle of life around my heart. My body was limp, my hands numb and my dreams stable in my ability to change from one to the other depending on the depth of their excitement. The world of life had left me, and the world I created took over. It was everything that felt good: laughter, smooth bare skin relaxed against mine, long curls of black hair scented with honeysuckle and green apples laying soft and cool on my face, the fire flickering, splashing flashes of orange over my thoughts in the darkness.

Caught comfortably in the web of my high and exhaustion, my body was gone from me. I felt nothing but the weightlessness of bliss floating inside me. I was free.

Over my closed eyes, a layer of gentle blue built in brightening scales and began to pull me back. I fought hard to hide my awareness of its aborning. Now she came and went. I released the clasp of my hands from my chest trying to ignore the rush of stinging blood lighting up the tips of my sleeping fingers. Soon I found my place again, but more light came, and I was so grateful for the opportunity to see one of the few enormously beneficial sights of reality.

Fighting through the thickness of a slimy high dream, the seal of my eyes broke loose and the light that fell into me was stretched with nameless hues of orange and blue, and in that moment, I was so in love with life – and suddenly, for just a moment, I didn't want to leave it. An early rising full moon over the bay was nothing less than a miracle to me. It was bigger than everything that was myself, my questions, my ability to answer them, and my ever wondering about who made it all real. It was someone I could never be and it was no one that I knew, but it was something strong and large, tough, but more loving than I could understand. I knew, for I was bathing in the light of one of His greatest gifts. How could it be that something so large, so beautiful, so bright could still have no life? Its surface cold and gray, dusty and without water or air. Maybe I'd live long enough to die of suffocation should I be fortunate enough to dance freely about a glowing bed of moon dust in the utter absence of gravity. What a way to go. Angels float. I figured I better take my chances. Always take your chances – otherwise, you're not living. You're dead. A man put an American flag on the moon. It's there. I've seen the fucking pictures. Look at what I done.

A sharp light slashed my view. The spotlight combing the still sea grass stopped as Pop spotted me. The light went off and I stood and moved toward the shore. My skin burned with anxiety, but it felt good to make my way into the cool water. I washed the mud from my body, but left it dried on my face as I could hear the mosquitoes steadily swarming my head, searching for a spot of exposed flesh in which to drill.

I handed my gear to Piggy, then the stringer holding three beautiful redfish. Piggy giggled with excitement as he showed them to Pop. I climbed up into the boat and waded through the thick odor of shrimp. Without asking, I dug into Pop's cooler for a beer.

"Make it a double," Pop said.

Clicks and spews, his beer was always ice-cold. "Thanks for the lift," I said, as I made my way to the old cleaning table on the starboard side of the stern. Under a small light, Piggy was already cleaning the fish.

"Pig, I'll take care of that. You've worked hard enough today."

"Ain't no problem, Mr. Jax. Go ahead up and get you some wind."

"You sure you don't mind?"

Piggy turned and looked me in the eye. "Mr. Jax, you look like you need some rest. When you look that a way, it means the man above trying to tell you somethin."

"Piggy, it's just the mud. I feel just…"

"Mr. Jax," he interrupted, "I don't want to be the cause of no man not listening to his creator, whether that man wanna listen or not. Now go on, get you some wind." Piggy turned his attention back to the fish, but I was frozen, feeling as though he had just stolen a glimpse at my soul. He looked right through me and for a moment I felt naked and weak, exposed like a withering cottonwood in December's desert.

I made my way to the bow of the boat and let the night winds and cold beer wash away the pain, the physical pain, anything emotional was already dissolved in the boil of booze and drugs and physical exhaustion. This was my time to be free again. I was in good hands. I felt the angels around me in the night sky. The appreciation overcame me, and I smiled beneath quiet tears. The diesels churned, chopping a wake behind us, leaving another day of life and madness bubbling in its fizz.

supper

It was almost nine o'clock by the time I pulled into the parking lot of Louie's restaurant. I'd stuck around the marina to help Pop and Piggy unload their catch and ready Freeloader for its morning voyage. Pop was kind enough to let me pick a few dozen shrimp for my keeping. I grabbed a handful and tossed them in a plastic grocery bag filled with ice and two large redfish filets on the half shell. With such little time, I went straight to the restaurant.

From the parking lot I noticed how unusually crowded the place was for a Wednesday night. Wednesday. Wed Nes Day. I just didn't get it. There must be something behind it: If not, it would be a tremendous disappointment. Weddings, parties, flowers, children dressed in miniature formal wear, red rose petals falling soft on marble floors. These images saturated my mind again. Growing up, I had always considered Wednesday hump-day, a day that in my high school years had an exciting and pleasurable meaning. What a waste of thought thinking of it as the middle of a work week. I figured if you're counting the days until you get a break from the life you live, you're not living your life.

I sat in the Jeep watching more and more people arrive. They disembarked from clean new cars, clad in sport coats and new-fangled sailing shoes, high heels and diamonds and gold, thirsty for vodka and chardonnay, hungry for calamari and lobster tails with garlic butter sauce – and all served on white tablecloths with crystal goblets sparkling in the flames of white votive candles.

I was in no mood to mingle with a swarming sliver of tipsy reality, but I could get that way, and that's what I did. I pilled and drank and smoked until the chaos behind the stained glass windows drowned its way into a colorful mixture of muffled slow motion reality sliding down the barnacle-coated pilings, into the bay and out to sea with the lowering tide melting my mind.

After several minutes of slow, deep breathing, I felt fairly certain that my gut was not going to evict its holdings. For reassurance, I tore the head off a shrimp and peeled away its shell down to the tip of its tail. With my lighter, I warmed away the raw texture and swallowed it. This helped, but I wanted hot food and neat scotch. I grabbed the plastic bag of fish and shrimp and melting ice and made my way inside.

As I entered the foyer, I stopped and held open the door for an elderly couple. The woman looked almost scared. Her red-nosed husband just smiled and thanked me. He was thinking nothing but bar. I could see the lost longing in his polite, bored, red eyes.

Once I was inside, the façade of swirling commotion that I saw from the Jeep was now whisked away with the noise of dishes clanking, loud, obnoxious laughter and cigar smoke. Then, like a nail in my ear, I could hear the high-pitched voice of Louie as he kissed an array of ass. Quickly sucking money out of the customer's wallets and into his. "Yes sir." "Great to see you again." "Enjoy your meal." "If you need anything, anything at all, just let me know." "Thanks for coming in." "Y'all drive careful." Louie was an ass-kissing genius. To watch him in action was both impressive and sickening, but the way I saw it, if you're good at something, you might as well stick with it. How nice to be compensated for one's talent. Is that happiness? I reckoned maybe, but not necessarily.

As I took a seat in the corner of the room, Khan, an elderly Pakistani man who had been a busboy since the restaurant's opening day, greeted me with a welcoming smile and a double MacAllen 25. I held him soft on the neck and leaned down to kiss his beautiful olive bald head. He was such a soft man. A gentle man. A man working to care for his family far away. He was what a man should be. I was his opposite. But Khan and I connected in a spiritual way. We both knew it wasn't easy. "How you have been, Mr. Miles?" he asked.

"Much better now my friend," I answered, draining the scotch. "How boutcha, Khan?"

This was sort of unfair to ask Khan since English was not his first language, but I rationalized it by not knowing if the question itself was English. Khan was smart. He just changed the subject by telling me I looked as if I'd had a "good fish day" – then he took back my empty glass.

"I'll get you another."

I loved Khan. He always made me feel as if I were sitting in a very comfortable chair. Soft leather. Leather the color of whitetail fur in winter. Wet sand in the soft evening glimmer of the sun. Cowboy leather.

I was sitting, but not in a Khan chair. It was a high back chair with shiny wooden arms and genuine maroon vinyl. I felt like I should have been in some meeting with a bunch of other uncomfortable people devising ways to sell something that ultimately ends up being utterly useless to mankind. A refuse machine. It was tight and awkward, but more awkward were the odd looks I continuously received from the herd waiting to attack the trough. At first, I excused it as paranoia from the weed or the wet plastic bag dripping on the old wooden floors, but the scorn was real. It was the woman for whom I had held open the door. She looked at me then snickered something through the gray sag of another woman's ear. Like a virus in a tribe, it jumped one by one to others nearby. Dead dominoes. More people looked at me then whispered among themselves. Certainly, I was underdressed, but I wore the same thing every day because that was all I had: flip-flops, fishing shorts made of a quick drying combination of cotton and nylon and either a t-shirt worn thin with slits and holes or a fishing shirt with multiple pockets made of the same material as my shorts. This was my uniform, my costume, my garb du every jour. It was functional, and even more comfortable. I had no reason to wear anything else and didn't want one.

More stares came, and I decided it was time to address the issue.

"Are my balls hanging out again or what?" I asked loudly.

The foyer fell silent as Khan entered with another double scotch.

"Khan, I love you for so many reasons."

Khan nodded and slipped quickly back to work as he was well aware that Louie objected to my drinking the best single malt in the house, especially since it was on the house.

I stood and walked toward the hostess' stand. The silent, blue herd kindly parted a path without my asking. Louie stood behind the podium like the great statue of the Inflamed Hemorrhoid, furious and terminal with anguish, unable to do a damn thing. I handed him the dripping bag of fish and shrimp, swigged a hefty mouthful of my drink and leaned over to where our noses almost touched.

"It's tough to be stuck between a rock and a hard-on, ain't it, Louis?"

Without a word he handed me the keys to his office. This meant to go upstairs and wait for him. Immediately. Please. As I turned toward the staircase, there was nothing but a pack of silent, disgusted glares – pushed cattle in the rain.

"You people look as though you've never seen a junkie before." Suddenly, I realized this was the perfect opportunity to flatter Al Pacino as Tony Montana in the great movie *Scarface*, so I just let it rip in a horribly off-key Cuban accentuated slur. "That's right. Take a good look at da bad guy. I'm da bad guy. Now you have someone to point your *fucking* fingers at and say, 'dat's him, dat's da bad guy.' But I'll tell you dis," I tugged my shirt proudly, "dis the last time you see a bad guy dressed like dis."

As I spoke to the crowded silence, I began to realize that I wasn't even remotely close to sounding like either Tony or Al. Had I completely butchered the lines? Now what to do? My answer was to improvise, loudly. Stick to the script. I pointed at Louie, "His wound is so polluted, I can't even have a little baby wit him. Give me another quaalude... I mean give *him* another quaalude. He'll love me again tomorrow." That was it. That was all that I could think of, except the indomitable way he took that woman into his life because he knew she was *the* one. I grabbed ten seconds of silence and looked into the bulging eyes of my wrinkled audience. "Should anyone desire my presence, I'll be in my cell."

Ascending the stairs, I felt sorry for Louie. He was going to need a barrel of motor oil to heal his chaffed lips after that little episode. I could already hear him apologizing and offering free drinks and appetizers. Poor Louie. All my life, he'd been the easiest book for me to read. I wondered if everyone had a Louie. I knew I did. I knew every precious minute of it.

In Louie's office, I knew exactly where to look. On the top shelf behind his desk were meaningless old accounting records bound in white three-ring binders. There were overstuffed manila folders bound by thick rubber bands stacked four or five high. It was typical Louie, a spot so common and uneventful that not an eye in the world would think anymore of it. Louie's was so enjoyable in fiction, but sometimes I was sad about the non-fiction inside him that I was always aware of but rarely allowed to touch.

I pulled down the stacked folders and peeked behind the binders, then cautiously pulled out a glass picture frame and set it down on Louie's desk. It was all there: four small lines, a razor blade, cut straw and a mound of coke set to the side waiting to replace the lines that would be sucked away. "This is pathetic," I said, disappointed. "What's the point?" I took the razor blade and scraped the four lines into two fat rails. "If you're going to do it, do it." A heavy stir swallowed the cold white crystallized oxygen. It was hailing grains of energy inside a body that just longed for sun. Wow. I was lit-up like a frozen strike of lightning. They have those. I've seen the fucking pictures.

I got on the phone at Louie's desk. There were buttons everywhere, assorted colors, abbreviated words that made no sense, lights flashing, blinking, fluttering, chaos in a plastic box. I looked for the one button labeled "Bar." It wasn't there. I decided to just start pressing buttons until someone answered.

"Thank you for calling Louie's Waterfront..."

"Yes ma'am, I'd like a double MacAllen 25, neat, and your gorgeous body wrapped around me."

"What are you doing up there?" Celeste asked.

"Waiting to smell your skin."

"Yes sir. I'll send it up right away."

At that, I snorted two more rails and put the coke in Louie's top desk drawer. My shirt landed draped over a small printer – my shorts stack-fallen, wrinkled on the floor as I simultaneously stepped-out of both my shorts and flip-flops.

I sat naked at Louie's desk, my feet propped comfortably on a stack of papers. Looking around his office, I sensed only stress and lack of time – not for me, but any poor soul that might inhabit a place like this day after day. Lying beneath it all was a streaming sense of organization, purpose and time.

It was as though I were looking at a painting that I hated but was eternally damned to view. Attached to the inside of the door was a full-length mirror. This made me sick, and I quickly wondered if I had any mirrors back at my apartment. More damaging to my sight was the contents of the shelf that held the stereo, which continually played classical Italian music throughout the restaurant. I thought of putting on the baseball game, but was sure that this would prompt Louie to interrupt my forthcoming rendezvous with Celeste.

That thought drained away as I noticed the foray of toiletries neatly placed next to the stereo. There was aerosol deodorant spray (several different brands), mouthwash, assorted brands of expensive cologne, two hairbrushes and a can of hair styling mousse. I shook my head in disgrace and peered at all the notes attached to the corkboard above his desk. There were employees' names and phone numbers, letters of appreciation and complaint, various types of foods with prices and quantities beside them. It was confusing, but, looking through Louie's eyes, I could feel the organization tighten around me. I noticed two yellowed papers stuck to the bottom of the board – both were in my handwriting. The first quoted Richard Nixon addressing his White House staff for the last time before resigning. It read as follows: *"Always give your best. Never get discouraged. Never be petty. Always remember, others may hate you, but those that hate you don't win unless you hate them, and then you destroy yourself."* I had not read those words in quite some time. Strangely, they meant more to me in written form than when he spoke the actual words to the country on television. Maybe that was it. Someone had the balls to say it. I guess it just shot a hole through my soul that never healed. The other note was a bit more effortless. It read: W*hat are you really doing?* I recognized my handwriting, but had no recollection of ever writing or placing either of the notes there.

A slight knock sounded at the door.

"Un paseo," I called.

As the door opened Khan entered with a heavy glass of scotch.

"Khan!" I said with a smile. "You have brought me a gracious gift. I love you more than you will ever know."

I stood and hugged him. He was a bit stiff but smelled of welcoming cologne.

"Are you okay, Mr. Miles?" he asked, never taking his eyes off mine.

Grabbing the drink from his tray, I raised it, "Never better. And your wife and children – are they doing well in Pakistan?"

"Very well, Mr. Miles," he answered quietly.

Walking toward the door, I followed him. As he shut the door, I stopped it before it closed and handed him the silver can of styling mousse.

"Please dispose of this evil at your earliest convenience my friend."

He smiled.

"Yes sir, Mr. Miles. It would be my proud pleasure."

He took the can and placed it into the pocket of his starched white apron.

"I love you, Khan." And patted him on the ass.

He descended the stairwell wearing an anxious, unsettled smile.

As I shut the door, the reflection of my naked body in the mirror froze me. How long had it been since I had seen what

everyone else was seeing? I looked as though I were wearing
a dark brown suit of skin and bones. My forgotten mask of
dried mud was secondary to the sight of the shriveled man in
the mirror. He was a stout young Marine just yesterday, a
linebacker bursting with energy, a pitcher with a tailing
fastball, a knee-buckling curve and always the beautiful girl
in his arms at the end of the game.

How age had suddenly crept upon me. I looked old and
withered and damaged. It was happening too fast. There
were too many changes. The reality of it all was foul and
offensive to my spirit. Fuck it. One more rail. And so it
was.

Louie's office door flung open like a sail caught by a mighty
gust. It shut swiftly, too, but without a sound. Louie wanted
no more trouble.

"Do you ever feel like you're wearing a straitjacket?"

He said nothing about my being naked, nor did he mention
the *Scarface* masterpiece downstairs. He glanced behind me
at the shelf, "Is it all gone?"

"Nothing goes to waste."

"You fucking asshole."

As he started in, I pulled the picture frame from his desk
drawer and held it in my hand.

"It would be an even greater waste were I not to share with
my best human friend."

His shoulders dropped with relief. He opened a small door
and grabbed a clean, neatly folded white apron. Taking the
frame from my hand, he replaced it with the polyester apron.
It felt like parched driftwood in my hand.

"Put this on."

I rotated my hand and the apron fell to the floor. "Sorry, but no."

Louie retrieved the apron and tossed it into my lap.

"You're out of control," he said, snorting a line. "Put the apron on. Please, just put it on."

"We're all out of control if you think about it."

"Don't start."

"I already have."

"Well, stop. I don't have much time. Barbara's coming in for dinner tonight."

"I rest my case. And, yes, I'd be delighted to join you."

"Don't even think about it."

"Again, Louie, I already have. After all, I caught the fish."

"You'll be eating up here. Alone."

"I'm afraid that's not possible, Louie. There's simply not enough room in here for the three of us. Besides, I miss Babs."

"Well, she doesn't miss you."

"She knows not what she misses, my friend. For her sake, she never will."

"Whatever. Here."

Louie pushed the frame in front of me and away went a rather substantial portion of the powder pile.

"For crying out loud, you wanna take it easy! I'm the one who pays for this shit. Jesus Christ!"

"Your arm must ache from all the twisting. And Jesus is not involved."

"Why are you naked?"

"I was told this is the way I come out."

There was a knock at the door.

"Entra! Entra!" I immediately called.

Louie scrambled like a scared chicken, snatching the cocaine from my hand and hiding it away. Celeste entered. A glass of scotch glistened under her fingers like rain dripping from freshly woven strands of ivy. Quiet. Intricate. Peaceful. Greatly underappreciated.

"What the fuck are you doing?" Louie snapped in a near whisper.

She walked past him toward me.

"I'm bringing up his drink."

"He doesn't need another drink."

"He ordered it."

She handed me the glass of scotch, and I took her hand and kissed it. It was as soft as water. I pulled her down into my lap and kissed her neck and ran my tongue up behind her ear. It was human honey warming in my mouth, honey straight from the old ranch, jarred by the sun beaten hands of my

Indian grandmother, straight from the days I had too long forgotten. It tasted of life just before it turns toward death.

Louie stood perched with his fists at rest on his round waist. He sighed and stared at the two of us.

"You can go now."

I tightened my grip on her tiny waist as she attempted to stand.

"Would you like to join Louie and Babs and me for dinner?" I asked, straining just slightly so I could look her in the eye. "There's plenty for everyone."

"I'd love to, sweetie."

"No," Louie barked.

"But I have to work."

"No. You have to live and love. That's all."

"I wish it were that simple, Miles."

"It is."

She kissed me and said that she'd be back. Louie was about to let her have it, but she beat him to it.

"I'm going to get a wet towel for his face."

She spoke faintly as though they were talking about the old man in the room, who was too far gone to understand or count or do much of anything anymore. Maybe I should have been embarrassed, but it never came to me. It felt good to know that she cared. And she was lovely as she disappeared, the door closing behind her, but it stopped just short of closed because Louie demanded a Bacardi rum and Diet Coke when she came back. The door pulled shut. The ivy and all its splendor went away, but the divinely human taste of her still splashed in the stir of my mind.

"You're not going to fuck her in *my* office."

"But of course I am. Can you imagine a more lifeless spot? Look around. This place needs love, Louie. Do you have any crackers in here?"

"What the fuck do you want crackers for? Your dinner's almost ready. Besides, you've nearly snorted an eight ball since you've been up here. How can you be hungry?"

"I'm not. Never mind."

He was beginning to step on hallowed ground. I pulled the coke from the drawer and set it on his desk then drank from my glass. In his eyes, I saw the wonder fade into more immediate motivations. Louie diced and lined and snorted with the caution of a surgeon, then immediately went to his reflection in the mirror. He tucked at his shirt. He pulled at the waist of his slacks. He turned to look at the backside of himself. He brushed at his slacks and pulled on his sleeves revising imperfections that I could not see. He was making sure that the world was going to get what it wanted.

A tone sounded from his phone. I reached quickly for the receiver, but he charged me and took it from my hand.

"What? Okay."

He pushed two buttons on his phone that immediately changed him from an avid ass-kisser to the finest ass-kissing machine the world had ever known.

"Hey there!"

He spoke with such sudden excitement that the obedient sound in his voice made me bend down for another rail, but his hand gripped me by the shoulder, denying me the drugs. He listened nervously. When he spoke, it was nothing more than pleasure engineered on demand, and I felt the mud dry and crisp on my face.

"Okay. Be careful. Yeah, the Ben and Jerry's is in the freezer. Love you, too."

He hung up the phone, and I knew that my mask was better for so many reasons.

"Barbara'll be here in twenty minutes."

"Fascinating," I said with a smile, implying that he need not mention the obvious.

He looked at me, frustration seeping up red over his puffy olive cheeks. It was almost too easy, and I had grown tired of watching him suffer in fear of me and what I might do next. Louie was an easy target because I knew him so well. He either dreaded the sight of me or laid open his arms and let me scrape at the rusty iron gates around his soul. It was always one or the other. There was no middle ground. It rarely appeared as such, but it was always me who decided where we'd be. The mud on my face tightened around a big smile.

"I don't know how you do it, Louie, but you do and you do it well."

Like a warm blanket covering his worries, I could feel a sense of relief wash over him. He pulled a chair up to the desk.

"Miles, you're the one who said it was people like me that made life interesting for people like you."

"I never uttered such horseshit in all my life."

A jolt of uneasiness fired through the diminishing brown irises in his eyes. "Did I?"

I smiled again and he came back, arms opening. We each took a snort off the picture frame and I asked him what he had done that day and inquired into the people he had encountered. They were just names to me. I had heard them before, maybe even met a few along the way, but they too were cut from the same cloth as Louie. The sight, the feel of my fabric was not desired within their weave. This never bothered me. I had always considered it a blessing not to be included. It unintentionally gave the distinction more to me than to them. To receive without request is to truly receive. And I did once say that people like him made life interesting for people like me. I meant it, too, but not in the way he understood it, and it was perfect that way.

Louie gave me the details of his day, and we laughed together and found our way to the reason behind our friendship. When he stopped talking, I asked for more. There was always more. I knew this because he would speak to no one as he spoke to me – unafraid, free of judgment, real. And, for a while, we walked around the rusted gates and drifted on the moat below them. I felt the nearness and tried hard to remember the things he said. It was this side of Louie that I liked to remember when I was alone in the water and thinking of life and people and the reasons for it all.

"Have you talked to Fuckel yet?" He meant Finkel, my agent, to whom Louie had recently taken an acute disliking. I had stopped answering his calls some time ago, so Finkel started pestering Louie with several daily calls from Chicago.

"Not as of late." I really didn't want to talk about it, but I knew I had set myself up for Louie to dig.

"He just wants an update on your progress."

"He wants money."

"That, too, but can't you just tell the guy you're making a little headway and get him off *my* ass?"

"I can do that. What's the number?"

"It's right here."

He sifted through some papers on his desk and handed me a blue notepad. On the back was written Finkel's name and phone number. There were ink strikes in stacks of four with the fifth slashed diagonally through them. I counted thirty before it occurred to me. "When did you start counting?" He said after four days. I rolled my eyes in amazement at Finkel's relentlessness. I dialed the number and waited.

"Did you talk to that sorry fuck?"

Finkel's voice came in loud, ignoring any sense of greeting or manners.

"You kiss your mother with that mouth?"

"Miles, is that you, man?" In the background was the noise of cold people enclosed in a small, hot room. Finkel was either eating dinner in some crowded Gold Coast shithole or working over publishers at a stuffy literary gathering. He did nothing else.

"Where the fuck you been, I'm worried sick about you. We're real far behind schedule, Miles. What ja got for me, man?"

"I got this. You'll get it when you get it. In the meantime leave my friend alone. One more call and everything burns."

I hung up the phone just as Celeste knocked on the door. Two more drinks and a warm rag. She did the same thing in bed. She was wonderful.

Louie didn't seem to notice that Celeste had begun cleaning the mud from my face. Her touch was gentle. With great care, she unveiled the sunburned skin on my face. She said I needed lotion and left again. I thanked her.

"He's gonna call back," Louie said, disappointed.

"Have I ever lied to you?"

"No. But you can't burn it."

"I can."

"But you won't."

"I will."

"You're only fucking yourself if you do."

"Not necessarily."

"What does that mean, Miles?"

Celeste came in without knocking.

"Louie, Barbara is here. She's on the deck. I told her you were on the phone."

He seemed not to notice her again. Cool lotion on soft hands bled into my face, and I imagined the smell of fresh peaches.

"But he's *not* on the phone."

"It's okay, Miles, I didn't want her charging up here while you were naked."

"What do you mean, Miles?" Louie asked.

"Is twice in one day too much for her?" I asked in general.

Celeste took her hands slightly from my face and looked at me. I looked back at her. I looked at Louie. They looked at one another – then both looked back at me.

"Your wife's a Peeping Tom. You are aware of this?"

Celeste continued her therapy, a lock of black curl stuck to the edge of her lips.

"You're richer than blood, gal."

She smiled down at me and her eyes fluttered. I wanted her right then.

"How much have you got done since the Chicago deal fell through?"

Louie was not giving up.

"There's no need for code. She knows about Lauren."
Celeste said nothing. She did know. She didn't care.

"How much, Miles?"

"Zero."

"Nothing?"

"Two words. Same meaning."

"Miles, they're gonna fuck you to death."

"I was hoping Celeste would be the one."

"I'm serious, Miles. You can't lie to them. They're gonna find out."

"I didn't lie."

"You said you'd burn it. What's that?"

"That's the truth. I will. If he calls again I'll burn what I have. They have the same thing. No harm done."

"Not a fucking word?"

I looked at him as though he was the only other person on the face of the earth. And he knew.

"You really haven't, have you?"

He looked at me with great disappointment and trouble in his eyes. Celeste stopped and sat still in the silence. Louie stood and walked toward the door.

"Lauren's fucked you up and now the bitch is fucking up everyone around you."

The door slammed behind him. Celeste sat on the straddle of my lap.

"He's not very happy," she said.

"Why should he be?"

She smiled and kissed my forehead. I put my hands behind her ears and pulled our lips together. We kissed hard, then harder. I reached between us and unbuttoned her blouse at the bottom, pushing it up above her breasts. She resisted a little, but I put a firm hand on her back and she pulled her panties from under her skirt, my lips never leaving her breasts. She guided me inside her with one hand and held the back of my neck with the other. She gasped, and her eyes fell back. I was in her. We were one. It was warm and soft, and we rocked together with our lips sealed. Her hair seeped between our faces and, in the denial of its sweet scent, I bathed and swam and drowned in warm peach brandy flesh.

...

In a dream, I sat on the shore of the beach and spoke to a small child building a sand castle. He was a handsome young boy of six years with keen focus and silent determination. I said things to make him laugh, and he shied away smiling. His front teeth were missing. His hair was blond and cut short. He liked baseball and football. When I asked if he liked to fish, he said no.

"Why don't you like to fish?" I asked.

He said just cuz. I asked him what he wanted to be when he grew up. He said he didn't want to be anything, and I told him that was a very good answer. I sat and watched him mold buckets of wet sand with his little hands. At times, his tongue poked at the side of his mouth. His concentration was extraordinary and, at times, proved to be his downfall for, as he stacked and carved at one area, another would dry in the sun and crumble. It happened several times. I tried to warn him, but couldn't. He was thinking. When he noticed that the sand had fallen, he just said uh oh. I asked what his name was. He said paw. "Your name's Paw?" He said no. He jabbed his finger into the sand and carved out the spelling of his name. His name was Paul. I watched Paul for a bit longer – then my eyes were drawn to the surf. The water rose in tall green looping curls, folding into themselves, crashing the shore and bleeding upward a bubbling salt soap fizz. The rise of the waves stretched thin the water, and sunlight filtered in like x-rays revealing the schools of fish passing through. I stood and walked past Paul. "I'll be fishing," I told him and stepped toward the water. It was cool and light on my feet. I stepped in further and was soon waist deep. The sun was coming to evening set and the sky was all breeze without cloud. The silhouettes rose and fell with each break and I was standing in their midst.

"You need to come back from there."

It sounded like Paul's voice, but he was minding the castle, his back to me. I moved to deeper water where the fish were thick, brushing my legs with their passage. The urge to cast was churning inside me, and I reached for Old Faithful. I didn't have her. My tackle belt and fishing rod lay ashore where I had been speaking with Paul. I called to him but he could not hear me. Angry with myself, I stretched out my arms and fell back into the water. The noise of the wind fell silent to the pulse of the surf crashing around me. The fish swam near and around me. The rippling water rushed my face and fluttered on my back. I lay comfortable in that which I knew but could not see. I was just something buried in the bosom of something much more alive than myself. If only I could have swum away.

When I could no longer hold my breath, I pushed up to the surface and broke into the air. Saltwater crystals burst in the fizz, and the fizz grew and split at the crest of a whitecap, and the whitecaps grew because there were no waves, just wind and current. Paul was gone. The beach was gone. The sky was gone. There were no fish in the water, and rain came in from the side. I strained to see what I could, but it was cold. Only the whitecaps blistered the waters' surface. I felt life's end on my shoulder, and for the first time, I tasted the urge to turn to it and let it take me under. There were no fish anymore.

...

It was the white tablecloths beaming beneath candlelight in the fog of my peripheral that reminded me of that dream. They surrounded me as I waded through the restaurant toward the back patio. The noise had no definition. It was just the sound of a machine broken, but still grinding. People were silhouettes treading at my waist, laughing and eating and drinking. Dishes clanked, and voices blathered through mouths full of food. I was suffocating, as though I were walking through the aftermath stench of a warm Sunday morning massacre, the smoke still rising, holding like a fog of lost and decadent humanity.

At one point, I thought I heard my name being called. I told myself it was Paul calling me from the shore even though he never asked my name. I just kept walking. The water was calling me, pulling me with the current, forcing me to the salvation lurking atop its evening wallow.

With whatever was left inside me, I pushed open the tall glass doors that led to the deck outside. The salt air filled my blood like holy adrenaline. I stood still for a moment, pretending to look about for Louie and Babs. I needed air, and I needed it before I could take one more step. Khan passed by, then stepped back and asked if I was okay. I said yes. He asked if I wanted another scotch, and I said please, as the other one had spilled and fallen down my mouth. He didn't understand, but he went inside to get me another. Khan was a good man, a very good man.

...

What kind of self-sucking cock occupies the best table in his own restaurant? This kind of thing pissed me off. If you want the best seat in the house, go home and sit on your fucking toilet. Whether it was ignorance, stupidity or arrogance, there was no excuse for this behavior. Do you also honk at old people for driving slow? Do you consider the retarded less than human? Do you have the balls to sleep in the wet spot? You must understand that women don't stand just because there are no more seats. Get your lazy ass up. Give her your seat. If there is no seat, kneel and make one. Now I was sick and upset.

...

The air and the anger were invigorating and, without invitation, I gladly took my seat between Louie and Babs.

"Don't order the calamari here," I said. "I hear it's atrocious."

"Hi, Miles," Babs said. "We were just talking in private."

"I won't tell anyone."

Louie seemed a little stiff. "Are you sitting on a crab claw?"

"I thought you were eating in the dining room."

"I know. I can't believe you would actually think that. We talked about the three of us getting together for one last rendezvous."

"What do you mean?" Babs asked.

"I won't see the two of you anymore."

Louie rolled his eyes.

"Miles, you're leaving? I didn't know that! Yes! Yes! You definitely must have dinner with us!" She didn't care about Louie's reaction. It was like a fucking surprise going-away party that Babs was more than happy to host.

I looked out over the water and let the warm evening breeze tear away everything around me. My head began to nod. I couldn't straighten up, nor open my eyes. Drugs and booze and salt and redfish were putting me down like an old dog, and I drowned as quickly as I could. In the midst of it, I felt a separation coming, wide and open and clean with the polish of leathery, thorn-sharp insanity. The skies there were brilliant with colors nameless and beings brighter than light. Air so silent to the world that it dissolved away like reality sliding into a heavy high – lush and weighty like the smell of cold air meeting warm water under stars burning in a burst of free life. This place was bigger than anything that could ever find its way to me. Wild with spirit at darkness. Days afoot on the remains of an ancient ocean floor, the sky's blue holding me like mad, violent love. This place – it glided in a jagged puzzle of time and space and nothing but peace found me there. It came from a wash of clear rivers that wound in song and glitter, streams sewing a web around it all, keeping the evils away, nothing but love and things to come of which I knew not, but committed to all as though everything was gentle and kind, a harmony beyond mortal thought, a breath that filled with reason and thrived like stillness sleeping in the arms of unbound faith.

A noise, a dreadful, irritating noise pulled me back. When my eyes opened, it was Babs' mouth moving, words of no definition directed at me.

"Miles, are you all right?"

"I'm pretty good. Yourself?"

"No. You were just dozing off. Are you not feeling well?"

"I feel like I'm falling through the mind of a dream."

"Where are you going?" Louie asked, uninterested in any elaboration on dream falls.

"Yeah. Why haven't you mentioned this before?" Babs asked.

"There was no before."

"What do you mean?"

Celeste and Khan arrived at the table with a wonderful spread of redfish on the half shell, potatoes au gratin, asparagus, melted garlic butter and scotch.

"Beautiful," I said, looking up at Celeste.

Louie was boiling, but, with Babs there, he couldn't let it go. He had to sit there like a fucking child and be a good little boy. I reckoned everybody had to be something, even if it's nothing.

"We ordered something different."

"I canceled it," I said.

I took the basket of warm bread and unfolded the cloth that covered it. "Take this bread and eat of it. If you want something else – too fucking bad."

Babs dug in like a lost woman found. Louie sipped at his umbrella drink. I sensed a little gleam of discomfort spilling in.

I ate my fish to bones, drank my scotch in a gulp and stood up from the table. "Excuse me, but I must go now. Thank you for having me."

"Miles, where are you going?" asked Babs. "We haven't talked about your leaving. Don't we get to know where you're going?"

I was already a few steps away from the table. My insides burned like fire and acid, and I knew that it was only a matter of time before I would tumble or vomit or drop lifeless from it all. I didn't want to go back. And I didn't know where I was going. I just knew I had to go. Besides, Louie was my friend and I owed him much more than just my mere presence.

Standing at the table's edge, I had a vision of Paul drawing his name in the sand. Since Louie had not touched his fish, I asked Babs if she wouldn't mind seeing to it that Khan got the fish. She said she would.

"I want to thank both of you for your kindness. It is what I will most remember."

I walked away.

"Miles, are you leaving?" Babs asked, confused.

"Yes. I'm leaving."

And like the ghost of the mighty dark waters, I felt myself dissolve away.

dessert

Behind my Jeep, I lay beneath a large oak tree just having disposed of everything inside me. My gut wrenched until it held nothing. Then it wrenched harder, dry heaves and nausea that was too much. I fainted and slept in a bed of cool ivy. The sleep was good and dark, black and thoughtless. There was no pain, no time. Nothing but my body aching to be in the ground.

I awoke to the sound of a foreign voice. It was Middle Eastern and, as a cold rag ran across the fore of my head, I recognized Joshi's bony face. Light from the full moon filtered down through the oak branches, and I could see the emerald in his eyes and the sweat on his brow. Joshi was the valet at Louie's. Originally a chemical engineer from Iran, Joshi fled during the Iran/Iraq war. How he'd ended up here I'd known at one time, but not at that moment. Joshi helped me to the tree's painted white trunk where I could rest upright.

"There is blood, Mr. Miles. There is lots of blood."

I couldn't respond. Everything was spent. Only the cold bloody rag and the green eyes and the marmalade voice from a place far away kept me alive. "Dr. Roberts is eating inside. I will get him."

"No." It was as though I'd heard him say, *We'll take your freedom away.* "I'm fine, Joshi, thank you for helping me."

"But the blood, Mr. Miles, there's too much."

I grabbed his arm and held it. With my other hand, I took the rag from him and tossed it into the Jeep, "The blood will grow back. It's sort of kind and cruel that way."

With Joshi's help I stood and began to gather myself.

"Your gal?" I asked.

"I do not understand, Mr. Miles."

"Your girlfriend, how is she?"

"She's a fardking bitch."

"So your relationship is burgeoning?"

"I don't think so."

"Everything seems to be a circle, Joshi."

I spat in the ivy and saw the glisten of maroon blood and mucous on young green leaves. "Everything. There is no escaping it. So you see, it just can't end. Ever."

The emeralds beamed at me in a blend of both question and understanding.

"You're a smart man, Joshi. A good man, too. I wish you well."

I sat in the driver's seat of the Jeep and felt for my key still in the ignition. One key, I always felt, was one too many, but it sure beat the fuck out of walking.

"Are you sure I cannot get Dr. Roberts for you?"

"Absolutely certain, my friend. Thank you, Joshi. If I'm gonna a get a finger jammed up my ass, it's not going to be his."

Joshi smiled and asked if there was anything else he could do.

"Just ice water, please sir."

When he went inside, I started the engine just in case he didn't come out alone, but it was just Joshi with a large plastic pitcher of ice water. And it was as though I had been walking through the desert for my very last days, just me and dusty old Indian spirits and here, finally, there was the spring seeping up slowly from the tall grass, running down over the rocks and into my burning body as Joshi watched on, sweating a humid emerald glisten.

I pulled the pitcher away for a quick breath.

"Thank you, Joshi. You have a good heart, and I intend to take a piece of it with me."

"You are leaving here?"

"Yeah. I'm fixin to run on over to the tit bar…"

"No sir. No. I mean from this town, Mr. Miles. Are you going away from us?"

I looked at Joshi and drank some more water. The rest I poured across my forehead and onto my crotch. Ice gathered down about my feelers, kindling a fire of some kind. I handed him the empty pitcher and thanked him.

"I don't think you can ever really go away from a place without actually going to another. Which way did you go, Joshi?"

Joshi thought for a moment. "West."

"What did you find when you got here?"

"I found home, sir."

I smiled at my friend, my night's Samaritan.

"West sounds good to me, too. A man at home is living. Be well, friend."

I drove away from Joshi, and his sea green memory drained into my soul. I never saw him again.

tit bar

She said her name was Bonnie – short for Bluebonnet. Her
daddy had called her that. She was coastally beautiful. Her
hair was more violet than red, a slow drip of warm whiskey
bleeding into the pores of fresh felled mahogany. Her real
name was Starlan. She'd grown up there in Port Pescado.
Her brother, Wayne, was my high school friend, but he often
went by the name Peanut on account of the shape of his head.
But Peanut and I were friends no more. He'd always ached to
prove he was the biggest kid in school. Actually, I was. I
couldn't help it – I just sprang-up like a reed from the water.
One day we faced off at football practice. I kicked his balls
so hard he cried and stayed home for a week. Peanut and I
tended to avoid one another after that. Starlan remembered
me, but insisted that I call her Bonnie. I called her Starlan.

"Why not just use your real name? Starlan is a grand name
for a dancer."

"No, it ain't."

"Aren't you a tad green to be working here, Starlan?"

"Not anymore," she said waving her breast across my face.
"I remember you."

"How so?"

"I remember you playing football."

"How strange. I imagine Wayne might conjure up a similar
image."

"You wanna dance?"

"No."

"Why not?"

"Because I don't play games that I'm destined to lose."

"What do you mean?"

"I mean that I'm not going pay you to swing your tits in my face."

"You don't have to pay."

"I'm not going to."

She sat down beside me and pulled a small vile of cocaine from somewhere on her half-naked body.

"Do you party?"

"Please don't ask me that. It's such a disturbing mistreatment of a noun."

"Then, would you like to get high?"

"I am high. But yes, I'd like more, and I'd also like to fuck you if you're truly of age."

She took me by the hand and led me back to a darker corner of the bar appointed with large dirty sofas and low candle light. She showed me her driver's license in the soft red light. She was twenty-five. It made me feel old, but it also confirmed the fact that I would soon be sawing her in half. We snorted and drank, and she stroked my crotch until I was hard and deep inside her. She bucked and rode me from her straddle, her eyes rolled back white – mine red, sunken and hollow, waiting to end it by filling her with whatever was left inside me.

Just as the time was upon us, just as we smiled at one another, just as we ground harder into each other, just before she split in two, I felt a pain so great that it stalled momentarily prior to setting in like a burst of fire blasting up from my exposed testicles. I don't remember if I threw Starlan off me or if she was torn away by someone behind her, but I buckled as the pain and nausea climbed into the pit of my gut. Starlan was screaming in a fit of rage but I paid it no mind. I couldn't. If I could have, I'd have asked her to quit screaming as it was confusing and aggravating and only worsened the pain.

"Shut the fuck up, bitch!"

I recognized Wayne's smoke-hardened voice. He dropped a lock of whiskey-stained mahogany to the floor then grabbed me by the hair and pulled my head back. "Well how boutcha, Peanut?" His plum-knuckled fist slammed hard into my nose. I heard the cartilage crush like glass and fell unconscious, thinking how the new pain, strangely enough, relieved the old.

I came to at the tapping of a heavy metal object on the side of my head.

"Wake up, son!"

Wayne's smoker's voice was lofty with excitement as we tore down an old dirt road that I couldn't recognize through the miasma of my awakening. The cab of the truck was filled with the stench of cheap-cigarette smoke. Outside, just sea grass and the town lights dissolving in the distance.

I reached to roll down the window, and the pistol in his hand lashed across my ear. "Don't you fuck with anything in my truck, boy!"

I felt blood drip from my ear canal and down the side of my neck.

"I just need a little fresh air, Peanut."

He hit harder, splitting my scalp. Blood drew down the back of my neck. I fought hard against the pull of unconsciousness. Haze. Nausea. Smoke. Blood. And Peanut stirred-up in the blaze of a drunken pistol whip.

"Dead men don't need no air."

"I'm not dead."

"You ain't yet."

"That sounds oddly familiar."

"Shut the fuck up!" Wayne held the gun against the side of my head. "I'd do it right now if there wouldn't be no mess to clean up."

I turned and looked at him, the gun pointed between my eyes. He chugged at a plastic bottle of cheap bourbon.

"If you ain't scared now you'd better get that a way in a hurry."

This made him giggle in an evil, girl scout kind of way.

"I'm petrified, Peanut."

The gun slammed into my broken nose, part of the barrel catching my right eye, the skin slit and bled into my already bleeding ear. "I mean Wayne."

"I know exactly what you mean you good-for-nothin sumbitch."

I rolled down the window and, for doing so, took another thump to the head. Fuck him. He was too proud of his old Chevy to have to wipe my bloody body out of it. I leaned into the wind, drawing life from the thick salt air. Before too long, I began to recognize our location. It was the old road that led to Rattlesnake Point, a dead end at the edge of a forgotten cove where large shell reefs kept anglers away, and tall grassy swampland gave untouched refuge to gators and cottonmouths and feral hogs. As for rattlesnakes, there was only one. It was said to have been a few inches shy of eight feet long and had killed a soldier on a training exercise one hot day in the late 1920s. The other soldiers in the unit said that the snake, just from the force of its strike, had snapped the soldier's leg clean at the knee. They had shot at the snake before trying to save their dying comrade, but the great serpent vanished in the grass never to be seen again, taking with it a combat-boot-covered leg. Fact or myth, I had to agree with Peanut, this was a good place to kill a man.

"You mind if I have a snoot of that whiskey?"

Wayne didn't answer. I took that as a no.

"Is there some particular reason why you wanna kill me, Wayne? I think that kick to the balls right in the midst of me unloading in your little sister's ass was revenge enough. Don't you?"

"This ain't about no revenge ya arrogant bastard." Wayne stopped the truck and told me to get out. "If you run, I'll shoot ya."

"I thought you were gonna do that anyway."

"Fuck you. Get out."

I got out and stood in front of the truck as Wayne had ordered.

"Why do you want to kill me, Peanut?"

His swing was broad and came skyward down on top of my head. I was out before I hit the ground. As I came to, I could taste the dirt and blood in my mouth. Nothing tastes like

73

blood because it's not meant to be tasted, but the taste of it always means something. He drank from his plastic bottle and spat a mouthful of whiskey in my face. It stung deep in the slit of my eye.

"Your dead ass is gonna give me some justice. Me and the men like them men I work with ever day." He drew a last hit from his cigarette and flicked the butt off the side of my face. "The world's gonna be a better place without the likes of you in it. You and your fancy little book of bullshit and content for men like me."

"Contempt."

"What?"

"Contempt!" I said. "You ignorant fuck."

His boot came into my belly hard and harder. I vomited and spat and asked him if he knew a coonass by the name of...

"Shut the fuck up!"

From the ground I leaned on one hand and tried wiping the mishmash of blood and whiskey and puke from my eyes with the other. "You mean to tell me that you're gonna kill me because I don't work at the refinery?"

"You don't just *don't* work at the refinery. You don't work period. And you're a stuck-up asshole to boot."

"And all this time I thought it was because I was knocking the bottom out of your little sister's starfish." A quick crack sounded as this bought me a few healthy kicks to the ribs.

"Get up. I don't kill no man if he ain't standin."

"You've killed before?" I asked pushing myself to my feet.

"You heard me."

"I did. It was very *old west* of you, Peanut." I shouldn't have said it, but I did. The pistol whipping I received because of it sent me back to the ground where I vomited again and spat and tried to collect the bloody, whiskey-burnt pieces of myself. I could hear Paul's voice again. It told me I'd better come back from there.

"I've got money."

"It ain't gonna do you no good now."

"That's a good point, Wayne, but it might do *you* some."

"Nothin of yours is gonna do me better than what I already gots."

"Do you gots fifty thousand dollars, Peanut?"

"Fuck you."

"No. I simply refuse to do the whole family, Wayne, but I am offering you a trade." I made it to my feet bloody, bruised, broken and blurred. It hurt to breathe, but I knew Paul was right. "I've never put a monetary value on my life, but I reckon, in this situation, it might be worth fifty grand."

"You're lyin. I seen you around since you come back from wherever the hell you been. You ain't nothin but a bum. A fuckin born loser."

"You can put the barrel of that gun back to my head, and I'll take you to it right now."

"I ain't buyin it." Wayne spat on my feet and in his eyes I could see the slow wheels turning. "How'd a flake like you get aholt of that much money?"

"It's kind of a long story, but I can prove it to you." When I reached for my wallet, Wayne quickly jammed the pistol in the drizzle of my ear. "I got a letter in here from some folks. It's proof of the money they gave me. It's like a down payment for a project that I haven't been working on."

"So you're a fucking thief, too. Figures."

Wayne was suspicious. I asked him to go easy. I asked him this because I really did have the letter. I kept it in my wallet for some reason. Maybe I just knew they'd need it in court. As I tried to separate the waterproof seal, Wayne snatched the wallet from my hands.

"You'll see it in there. A folded piece of paper. White as snow."

Wayne pulled the folded white paper from my wallet and stepped in front of the headlights to see the words written. I watched his eyes roll slow across the page and felt his attention fall away from me and into the money words.

I leaped at the pistol in his hand. His wrist bones snapped in the night silence as I twisted his hand like a doorknob. I pulled skyward snapping his elbow. It popped like a semi-deflated balloon. I could feel the blood flowing in and out of my ear as I strained. Fuck that sorry motherfucker. I cocked my leg and blasted his shoulder out of its socket. He wailed as I stood trying to slow my breathing.

With the gun in my hand, I asked for my wallet back. He just moaned and cried like he did when we were kids. I felt déjà vu as I took it from his hand. The smell of freshly cut grass fooled my senses as I pointed the pistol down at Wayne. He covered his head with his good arm and begged me not to shoot. I did shoot. And in the silence of the aftermath, I could almost see the hot breath of a dying alligator condensate on the skin of Wayne's red neck.

Wayne pissed himself at the sight of smoke from the bleeding hole in the gator's head. "You almost shot me you crazy bastard!"

"I'm not finished."

"Don't kill me. Please, Miles, don't kill me. I wasn't really gonna shoot ya."

"Peanut?"

"What?" he answered, squirming in pain.

"You're probably the most ignorant person I know."

"You're right, Miles. You're right. Just, please, don't kill me. I'm hurtin bad dammit."

"If I aimed for you to die, I'd of let the gator have your sorry ass."

"Yessir…"

Before he could say any more, I fired a bullet through his kneecap nearly severing his leg in two. Wayne screamed from the pits of his gutless soul and cried like a mother over her cold, dead baby.

"Peanut?"

He just cried and squirmed and cursed and yelled for help.

"Peanut?"

"What!" he screamed. "What the fuck do you want from me?"

"I want you to quit bitchin for a minute so I can ask you a question."

"I'm bleedin to death, you asshole! Fuck you and your question!"

He cried and bled and screamed bloody murder.

I raised the pistol and fired again. Wayne twisted on the ground begging for his life. Another smoking hole billowed from the gator's head.

"Now he's got two holes in his head, and he's just as quiet as a corpse. You reckon we ought to do the same with you?"

"I'm hurtin bad, Miles. I need help. Please, Miles, don't do this to me."

"It's just pain, Peanut, that's all. It's just a word."

"What the fuck are you talkin about? Look at all this blood! I'm gonna bleed to death!"

"I've seen enough blood. What I haven't seen is any life coming from it."

"I don't need to hear this shit!"

I pointed the pistol at Wayne's crotch. "One more sound, Peanut, I don't care if it's the sound of you breathin cry, but, if I hear it, I'll take away any chance you'll ever have at procreation."

His teary eyes grew wide and bugged with confusion. He wanted to bitch and scream and piss and moan. He wanted to ask, but I stopped him.

"You can look it up at the hospital. You still got one good leg and one good arm. It's not too far a crawl."

"Miles, you can't leave me here. I'm gonna die."

"Then you'd better start livin. And righteously, too."

"Fuck you!"

"That's not a good start."

"You're a sorry bastard!"

"That's what they say, Peanut. Good luck."

I walked away.

"Miles!" He screamed my name over and over. "What about the question? Ask me the fucking question!"

I walked back and sat down beside him. "I've decided I don't want to waste it on you."

"Try me, Miles. Try me. Please!"

I looked at his leg and determined that his gun was loaded with hollow point bullets. They make a hell of a mess and that's exactly what his leg was: a dangling mess of blood and tendons and shattered bone. I didn't know whether he was going to live or not.

I made it back to my feet and pointed the gun down at his head. "All right, Peanut. Here we go. Do you believe in God? Is He the Almighty? Does He perform miracles? Can He save your sorry ass from me killing you?"

"Yes. Yessir, I believe He can."

"So you think it's His decision as to whether I pull the trigger or not?"

"No, sir."

"Then what do you mean?"

"I mean... I don't know what I mean right now, Miles. I'm bleedin to death, you crazy bastard!"

"Well, guess what, Peanut."

"What?"

"I do know."

I walked back to Wayne's truck. Before climbing in, I looked inside for a rag or something to help slow down his bleeding. There was nothing.

"Peanut," I called, "this is a very tidy vehicle. I reckon we all got our priorities." I took off my shirt and tossed it to Wayne, "It's a tad dirty itself, but it should slow down the bleedin a bit."

As I drove away, Johnny Cash sang "Folsom Prison Blues" on the radio. It seemed too ominous so I shut it off. On occasion, I could hear the screaming of Wayne wallowing in pain and blood and self-pity. I turned the radio back on. If I went, I went. Either way, nothing would ever stop me from enjoying The Man in Black.

dump truck

The dock at the channel was quiet, motionless, empty of life.
I had cut off the engine because it was noisy with the sound
of bogus thunder. Peanut had done something to the engine
to make it sound that way. Louder. Cooler. Tougher.
Something about headers or some bullshit. I didn't know. I
never wanted to know. That's what guys like Wayne did.
They'd rather lean on their trucks than stand on their feet.
Big, fat, hairy pussies. I never aimed to judge anyone, but I
was also well aware that I, myself, was not without sin. So
fuck em.

The engine rumbled again, though this time louder as I
stepped away. I wanted to see it crash into the channel, but I
couldn't run on account of my broken ribs. Though I did
thoroughly enjoy its smooth dive and the second or two it
took before the water broke, crashing open the night's
silence.

At the edge, I drank from the plastic bottle and watched the
old moaner drown away. The whiskey was terrible, but I
sucked the bottle empty, put it in a nearby dumpster and lit
one of Wayne's cigarettes with the lighter that was stuck
inside the plastic wrapping of his soft pack. It was
uncomfortable to inhale, but the nicotine felt good.

I sat and leaned against the dumpster. Just smoke rising into
the stars. I was tired and wanted to sleep. After nodding
away a time or two, I heard Paul's voice say that pain was
just a word and that I'd better get away from there. I stood,
lit another cigarette and walked away.

gone home

It was about a five-mile walk back to the Jeep. The mosquitoes were ruthless, and I vomited several times along the way. I tried rubbing dirt on my skin, but the ground was too dry and wouldn't stick. I should have never given that cocksucker the shirt off my back.

"Wayne Davis is bleeding all over old Rattlesnake Point. You might ought to hurry."

I hung up.

I drove to Celeste's house and parked the Jeep in her garage. Her car was gone, no purple anywhere. I walked another two miles to my apartment.

The purple was there on the street in front of Louie's house. Celeste was sitting in the dark on the bottom step smoking a cigarette. She didn't hear me coming. I held Wayne's pack of cigarettes out to her.

"These taste terrible but they came with a free lighter. Ain't that generous?"

She didn't take them. She stood and hugged me, and we walked up the stairs and went inside my apartment.

She cried when the light came on. I must have looked a mess.

"Who did this to you?"

"I did."

I sat down on the bed. Celeste washed my face with a warm rag. She went to the bathroom several times to wrench it.

She brought out some old bandages and told me I needed stitches and that she wanted to take me to the hospital.

"They should do x-rays. What if you're bleeding inside?"

"Will you take a bath with me?"

She gave in and said she would. While she ran the tub, I grabbed an orange and held it to my nose but could smell nothing. Under my bed was an old coffee can full of pills. I peeled the top away and found the three biggest, whitest painkillers I could and swallowed them with red wine from a green jug, screwed the top back on and carried it to the tub.

Steam rose up from the running water. Celeste sat naked on the edge of the tub. She was crying without sound. I kissed her beautiful black hair and tried to smell it, but I couldn't. I put the jug of wine on the floor next to the tub then took her hands – her wonderful, glorious hands and slowly sat her in the tub with me. The old claw-foot tub was big and tall and put us comfortably close. We faced each other, and I smiled at her until she felt better.

We both drank from the bottle. It looked so big when she drank, as if she were trying to eat a watermelon from the rind inward.

"That bottle's bigger than your head."

"Miles, your face looks like lasagna."

"That sounds delicious."

She leaned toward me and worked the rag over my face. Her breasts were wet. Her nipples hard. Her dark black pubic hair glistened just up from the water. She was the only part of my life that was soft and sane. I took the rag from her and threw it on the floor. She kissed me on my collarbone. I guess it was the only place she thought a kiss wouldn't hurt.

"Your dick's hard as a rock."

"Those nipples aren't exactly dragging the ground."

She stood and turned her gorgeous body around. She lowered down and guided me inside of her, gently leaning back on my chest. Her eyes, fine and sharp, looked back at me then rolled back as she settled around me. We sat still. Connected.

I held the jug for her while she drank. The swallows in her throat rolled like evening waves sliding back and forth over the wet sand. I drank heavy and hard. There was still plenty left. There would always be wine. Time was something different.

"Did you see the moon tonight?" I asked.

"I did. It was wonderful. It looked so heavy and lonely, yet so glorious and at peace. I thought, it gives and gives and gives, but gets nothing in return. It's kind of sad."

"I think we should do it a favor and blow it to pieces. Put that sucker out of its misery."

"We'll do that to the earth first."

"You're right."

We added more hot water and drank more wine and laughed and kissed, and I held her breasts in the fold of my arms around her. She never asked me what happened that night. It wasn't that she didn't care – she just knew I wouldn't answer. I loved her for being so kind. I could feel myself beginning to miss her.

"Will you come inside me?"

"I was just thinking that very thing."

And I did. We pushed hard against each other and fell into the flowing swells of hot orgasm. It was warm and snug and had never felt so right. And we fell asleep in the tub, coupled and happy.

...

In the morning, I awoke to Celeste shaking me, telling me there was a knock at the door.

"Fuck off!" I yelled. "That wasn't directed at you, pretty."

And she was pretty, just as she was always. When the door opened, the daylight came at me like an angry white lion. Through the swell of my eyes, I saw Louie standing behind the sheriff or one of his deputies. I didn't know which one. I didn't care.

"Will you please shut that fucking door?"

"Miles J. Jax?"

I recognized the voice. It was Steve Rich. Sheriff's Deputy Steve Rich. I kept my eyes closed. One I couldn't open anyway. Peanut had seen to that. Louie wouldn't shut the door.

"What are you staring at?" Celeste asked Louie.

"Not much."

"Fuck you."

I knew Louie's eyes would be burning a hole through her. His dick was probably hard, but I couldn't blame him, I could only stop him. I flung my half of the blanket over Celeste so she wouldn't feel so exposed. I lay there still, eyes shut, the sunlight warming my balls. I felt as though my withered body weighed a thousand pounds.

"Miles J…"

"You know it's me, Steve. Don't you recognize Bret and the boys from the locker room?" Steve had played football with Peanut and me. He was short and stocky. I supposed he still was, though the last time I'd seen him, he had decided to decorate his handsome face with a big, beefy, brown moustache. Little Man's Disease. It must be awful.

"Did you shoot Wayne Davis last night?"

"Don't answer, Miles," Louie said. "Don't open your fucking mouth."

"Yes. I shot his knee once and a gator twice."

"Did you steal his truck, too?"

"Technically."

"Technically?"

"I put it where it belonged, Steve."

"Where might that be?"

"Bottom of the channel."

I felt Steve moving closer to me. I pulled up and rested on the bend of my elbows. A cloud moved under the sun, and the weight of the morning light lifted from my eyelids. Steve was standing next to the bed when I looked up at him. "I'm not resisting, Steve, but if you touch me, I'll tear this fucking place apart with you in it." I leaned into the blanket wrap and whispered to Celeste, "Not you, pretty, you know that."

"You can't threaten me, Miles. Sides, you look like shit."

"Yes, I can, but I didn't." I took a swig from the wine bottle aside the bed. "Steve, you know I wouldn't threaten you, even out of uniform, but do I look like I want to be pulled out of bed and handcuffed?" He didn't answer.

"Hey, Louie?"

"What?"

"Either come over here and suck on my cock or quit fucking staring at it."

"I'm not!"

"Okay. You are, but I understand. You've always been somewhat perverted, and I can only guess that sex with Babs makes you feel like a necrophiliac."

Celeste laughed beneath her blanket wrap. Louie just stood there looking like a guilty necrophile. Steve smiled, looking away from Louie.

"Look, Steve, I know I have to go with you, and I will, but could you and Louie step outside for a few minutes? We were just fixin to fornicate."

Celeste giggled. Louie looked a bit more excited. Steve looked around the apartment, then down at me.

"I'll be downstairs, Miles."

They stepped outside and shut the door. I reached for the coffee can and swallowed down a handful with the rest of the guinea. Celeste climbed on top of me and wrapped the blanket around us. We kissed and smiled at one another.

"You're going away, Miles."

"Right now I'm here."

"You're still going away."

Tears dripped from her cheeks onto mine.

"Don't cry, pretty. It's just another door opening for you. Walk through it. Forget fear and live the life it brings you."

"Miles…"

"It's okay. Just hold tight to faith and things will happen as they're supposed to. Trust me."

She laid her chest gently down on mine. We made love without a sound. And when they took me out into the bright day, I knew I would forever miss the smell of her skin.

jail

For a junkie, the hardest part about a small town jail is the unsought sobriety. I received a two-year sentence, a year and six months for the knee shot and six more for the truck. It didn't really matter to me though. I knew that anything over two months was a life sentence.

I was supposed to be shipped to the state penitentiary in Huntsville, but due to overcrowding I was kept at the tiny four-cell jail in Port Pescado. It was old and quiet and clean. Other than a few weekend drunks from the city, I was its only long-term resident. They said I'd be shipped off as soon as a bed became available. That's like trying to stick a dry pumpkin up your ass. It takes forever.

For the first few weeks, I lay in my bed shivering with fever. Sometimes, it would come up too fast, and I would vomit blood clots into a toilet bowl slick with black diarrhea. When they asked if I wanted anything I always said the same thing. "Freedom and scotch." They never brought either.

My cell was much more organized than my apartment. Concrete floor, chair, small table, bed, toilet, sink. I was fortunate for my single, barred window. It was located high on the wall, but if I held onto the bars and pulled myself up I could see the bay. And that's what I did. In the morning, I watched the boats pass by. In the afternoon, I watched the wind stir up whitecaps. In the evening, I watched the boats return beneath a sky of flaming peach thunderheads.

Steve took the nightshift as jailer for overtime, and I think he sort of felt sorry for me. If I was feeling up to it we'd play gin and talk about how pathetic Peanut looked in court with his casts and bandages and still that old sour look in his eyes. Most of the townsfolk sympathized with Peanut – after all, he was a third-generation refinery worker, and I was just a Galveston transplant looking to cast my line in warmer waters. Peanut did look pathetic, just as he did grabbing his balls and screaming like a dying cat on the football field.

One night, it was raining hard, and the sound was soothing. Steve surprised me with a bottle of scotch that he pulled from his pants. The cards shuffled, and the booze drained inside me like loose honey.

Steve asked me the same questions over and over again, but I had never answered. But that night, with the bottle in my hand, I decided to accommodate him – somewhat.

"You and I are the only people here. Why did you hide the booze?"

"I don't know. You never know what's gonna happen. Who might see something. Who might show up for one reason or another."

"What a puss."

"Why won't you eat anything but oranges?"

"Oranges are a miracle."

"They're a fruit."

"They're a fruit miracle. They grow on trees and fall to the ground, or some poor Mexican picks them and ships them off. When I look at an orange, the first thing I do is squeeze it for texture. Then, I smell it for freshness. They come wrapped in a beautiful peel that if it were the color of sand, would be no different from our skin. They're like the most beautiful Christmas gift ever wrapped. You tear away the peel, and there you have it, a wonderful meal, prepackaged by nature in ready-to-eat individual slices. Except for our consumption, I see no other reason for their existence."

"And what about your visitors?"

"What about them?"

"You won't see any of them. Louie, Celeste and that attorney of yours. He comes at least twice a day, but you still won't see him."

"Have you told him that I've asked him to get fucked?"

"I do it every time." Steve looked at me as I drank. "He says he can get you out of here."

"He can't."

"How do you know?"

"I don't. I just know him."

"You don't look well, Miles."

"I live in a cage, Steve. Even dogs don't sleep where they shit." We sat silent for a moment looking at one another. "Why did you grow that moustache?"

"What?"

"What made you decide that you needed to add a moustache to your already handsome face?"

"What's that got to do with anything, Miles?"

"I'm just interested in the psychology of the mustached man?"

"You're trying to get me off track."

"It's a face mullet. That's what it is."

"Stop, fucker."

"It's reverse psychology. I really want a mullet, but I don't want people staring at me. Bullshit. Quite the opposite. You think to yourself that you're really gonna look hot and hip and the gals are damn sure gonna notice. If her brain is the size of a hayseed, you might pull it off. But gals will notice that you think you're so cute that you have to decorate yourself with ornaments. What are you, a Christmas tree?"

"Look who's talkin. Your hair is fucking filthy. When's the last time you bathed or even shaved? You're just wasting away."

"Just shave the stache, Steve."

"Fuck you."

"Speaking of me, I am not a model. I am me and nothing more. What's your point, Steve?"

"I'm not sure. It just seems that someone who lives…" He stopped talking. "Never mind. It's your life."

"There ya go."

"Fuck, Miles!" He slammed his cards on the table. "I read your book this week, *Shredded Thoughts of …*"

"I know the title."

"Well, anyways, it wasn't bad, Miles. I mean it was weird, and I didn't understand all of it, but there were things in it that sort of got me. It was like I had finally been able to say things that I never had the words for."

"I'm happy for you. And thanks for buying the book."

"Oh, I didn't buy it – Celeste let me borrow her copy."

"Fuck you then."

"What's wrong with you?"

"I've got heartburn."

"That's not what I mean, Miles. Why won't you let anyone help you?"

"Help me?"

"Yeah, Louie offered to hire an attorney, but you defended yourself."

"I was saving him money."

"Celeste brings food and writes letters, but you won't accept any of it."

"She'll stop coming."

"Well your agent won't. That guy's a hardnosed little fucker. He's rented a house on the bay. Did you know that?"

"That sounds nice."

"Fuck nice. He wants anything you've got, even if it's not finished."

"He wants money, Steve."

"Who cares what he wants? He says he can get you out of here. Why won't you let him try?"

I stood and grabbed the bars, pulling myself up to the window. The rain was hard and steady. The bay lay still with open arms taking in the fresh water. In the flash of a lightning strike, I saw the silhouette of a man casting a net from a pier. It was quick and seemed only a figment of my imagination. Then, it happened again. I saw the cast net swing open, the weights twirl in the light.

"What the fuck is that guy doing out there?" I asked.

"What?"

"There's some idiot casting a net off the Lincoln Pier."

Steve pulled himself up next to me. "I don't see anything."

"Wait for the lightning."

Lightning struck, and the net spun in a perfect circle splashing level into the water.

"That dude right there on the pier."

Lightning flashed again, and again the net was cast.

"See him?"

"Miles, there's no one out there."

Steve looked at me as he held on to the bars. He seemed disappointed. He let go of the bars and sat back down at the table.

In another flash the man was still casting. I kept watching, amazed at what I saw. In the transparency of the next flash, he was gone. I waited, but more lightning revealed the same – nothing, just raindrops crashing down, millions of tiny tidal waves harmlessly crashing into one another. One more flash, and all was dark – the jail, the streets, the pier, everything. But the casting I could still feel as if it were me standing there in the rain. Something other than my stomach was finally turning – my soul. I lowered myself to the floor and heard Paul say that I needed to leave from there.

"I'd love to."

The light from Steve's flashlight stung my eyes.

"You'd love to what?"

"What?"

"You said you'd love to. You'd love to what?"

"I'd love to fly like a red tail hawk. You know? Just soar above it all for awhile."

"Uh, yeah. Okay, I'm gonna see if I can get the lights back on." Steve stepped out of my cell and I called him back. "Yeah?"

"Will you please bring me some paper and pencils and maybe a light source of some kind?"

"Great timing, Miles. Fuck, man, how do you do it?" He paused, confused and bit irritated. "I'll see what I can find."

Steve walked away. I lied down in bed but felt no comfort. I was reeling with anxious energy like I hadn't felt in months. Something had suddenly stirred up life inside me. It felt strange, but familiar, as though it were something I had misplaced and couldn't find because it was always just before the scope of my sight.

Steve returned with a large candle on a metal plate, a ream of copy paper and a handful of sharpened pencils. He sat it all on the table, then pulled a small plastic pencil sharpener from his pocket and sat it by the pencils.

"Lights are out over half the town. I gotta go. The place is all yours until Sheila gets here in the morning."

"Oh Sheila, Oh Sheila, I just want to feel ya!" I sang.

"Miles, she's seventy-two years old."

"Come on, Steve. She's a cutie at heart."

"Fuck off!"

"I plan to," I said with a smile.

"See you tomorrow night. Don't burn the place down, huh?"

"Hey, Steve?"

He stopped just outside my cell, bar shadows cast upon him by candlelight. "Yeah, Miles?"

"If you come across any drunks tonight, just take em home, will ya? I don't want to be disturbed."

"You're fucking crazy. You know that?"

"Anything's possible."

I heard the front doors shut, his squad car start and pull away. Thunder rolled and shook. I went to the table and tore away the wrapping from the paper. For a moment, I stared into the candlelight, thinking. The cast net spun, water sprayed off the weights and fell into the bay. I took a swig from the pint, grabbed a pencil and started in.

...

It was just before dawn when I awoke. Had it not been for Steve's asking if I were all right, I would have slept for two more days. As it was, I believed I had only slept for a few minutes or so.

"Miles?" Steve nudged my shoulder until he saw my eyes open. "What the hell happened in here?"

I sat on the edge of the bed, rubbing my eyes. The lights were back on. Outside the window it was blue dark and still.

"Are you going to answer me?"

I looked up at Steve. He looked strange and scared. The cell was a mess. The floor was littered with pencil shavings, papers waded and torn, an empty bottle of scotch and pencils that had been worn down to a nub.

"I can't answer you."

Steve picked up a neatly stacked pile of papers from the table. The top sheet was blank. I watched him as he flipped through the pages. He would hold a page here and there and his eyes would roll across the handwritten lines. He kept flipping and flipping, and the sound of the paper made me ill. I jumped from the bed to the toilet and vomited. My gut spilled until I heaved dry, broken breaths. I fell to the cold concrete floor, trying to stay conscious.

Steve stood over me, my manuscript still in his hands. I reached up to flush the toilet, but he stopped me and told me to lie still. He looked at the bloody water in the commode and quickly turned away. Pulling the pillow from my bed, he placed it under my head, then took his handkerchief and wiped my mouth. I opened my eyes and saw him looking at the bloodstained handkerchief.

"I'll get you a new one," I said.

"I'll be right back."

Steve hurried toward the hallway. And though it took all that remained inside of me, I beckoned him back. His breath was heavy. He was very scared.

I raised my hands to him. "The script."

Steve handed it to me and ran out of my cell. As the sound of his running feet faded, I locked my arms around the stack of paper and thought of Celeste and me in the tub. Then faded away into a solid black nothing.

infirmary

Five days and six nights had passed when I finally came back
to the world. I could fight my way through the worst of
hangovers to get to Mud Cut, but the morphine drip plugged
into my hand was so strong that I could only stay awake long
enough to know everything had changed and that I was no
longer in jail.

At first, I dreamed I was opening my eyes, and Lauren was
there at my bedside, her hand in mine, her head on my lap,
her green eyes looking up at me as if she were finally home.
The visions of Lauren were strange and strong. Her voice
was swimming in my head.

"I love you so much," she said. Her lips on my forehead.
Her hands on my face. Her long, sandy brown hair brushing
soft against my closed eyes. Honeysuckle. Green apples.
Fresh peaches. Skin like dusk on the sea grass. A touch like
warm cotton water.

...

Some time had passed. I was unsure how much, but it was
enough for me to stay coherent and look at my surroundings.
The small infirmary held a total of five beds. Mine was next
to the window, farthest from the door. Someone was sleeping
in the bed next to me. The other three beds were made,
tucked tight and waiting empty. Why right next to me? I felt
as if I had gotten the best table in the house and then some
fat, obnoxious woman with screaming quadruplets decided to
take the table next to mine – trampling all over my sacred
solitude. But the guy was sleeping quietly. Hell, he may
have been dead. Even better – for both of us.

I wanted to stand and look around. I wanted to know what was happening, where I was, where my script was. I tried to sit up, but the pain ripped through my abdomen like a burst of fire from some place of evil and torture. I fell back sweating, feeling my mind's feet slipping off the edge of consciousness. Stones and dirt trickled down into some nowhere. I pulled back the sheet and blanket. Through the looseness of my gown I peeked at my belly. A row of metal staples railed a track up from my half-shaved pubic hair to the base of my sternum. They had cut me open and gotten inside. I was pissed. No one had the right to fight off my death with a scalpel and a staple gun. My life had become just that – a life. I wanted to live, then die – not live, then stay alive until I was dead. That's when I knew I would soon be leaving.

I found the nurse's call button and pressed until the door opened.

She ran into the room wearing purple flowered scrubs. She was round and short. I heard the sound of synthetic fabric scraping together as she approached me.

"Mr. Jax, you're awake!"

"Unfortunately…"

"I'll call Doctor Roberts."

"Wait!"

She tried to rush away, but I wanted answers. "Where the fuck am I? Who the fuck are you? And why is this fuck in the bed right next to mine? What's wrong with the other beds? Who cut me open? What'd they take? And where in the fuck is my manuscript?"

That little outburst exhausted me. I laid my head down on the pillow and tried to stay awake. The nurse said nothing to me. She adjusted my morphine drip, then went to the bed next to mine. I tried to keep an eye on her, but I was fading. She gently woke the person next to me and whispered to him. I was dozing, but I wanted to fight. I couldn't. The drip flowed and drowned me, and I fell away with the vision of Lauren moving toward me from the bed next to mine.

...

It was all real. Louie had reached Lauren and told her everything and probably some shit that wasn't true. She flew down immediately and had not left my side since the surgery. I was missing over half my stomach, about twenty feet of small intestine, the majority of my colon and my appendix. I suddenly had a question. If you don't need an appendix why do you have one to begin with? We are much too evolved physically to have a body part that just occupies abdominal space, then, inconveniently, becomes infected and costs lots of money that we don't have. My theory was as follows: We had yet to evolve enough mentally to discover the true purpose for the appendix. I wondered if Albert Einstein had his appendix removed. If not, I might have had a lead. And then I heard those words that I could never quite put together.

"You have stage four stomach cancer," Dr. Roberts said. "We got what we could, but there's more to be done. Only it can't be done until you gain some weight and strength."

Lauren sat next to me in bed. The good doctor said more, but I was looking at Lauren. Her green eyes were bloodshot, and swollen and troubled. She sat next to me and made the world fall away.

"Mr. Jax, are you listening to me?" the good doctor asked. "We have a lot of work to do and very little time in which to do it."

"How much?"

"More surgery, radiation treatment, chemotherapy…"

"How much time?"

"It depends on your cooperation. The surgeries could be done in a month, maybe weeks depending."

"No, dammit! When will I die?"

"It's hard for me to believe that you're still alive."

"That doesn't help."

He said my life expectancy was no more than two months tops, most likely less. Then he left. Lauren cried on my shoulder, and I took her beautiful face in my hands and kissed her. Her tears were warm with the taste of salt. Her skin the shore to my sea. I asked her to make love to me, and she did, gently and quietly. Beneath the white sheets, she slept by my side as I made my decision. It was simple, really – stay and die, or leave and live. A simple plan is the best. I had one. It would soon be set in motion.

...

Steve had locked away the manuscript at home in his gun safe. I called him before daybreak and asked him to drop it by. When he showed, he had placed it in a perfectly fitting white box with two large rubber bands crisscrossing in safety.

"Damn, Steve, you must be in high demand come Christmas time."

"I didn't want anything to happen to it." He looked at Lauren sleeping, at my side. "She must be exhausted."

"She had a headache. I gave her one of my painkillers. She needs the rest."

"The judge is reconsidering your sentence on account of your health situation."

"Well, that's thoughtful, but extremely useless. Where's Fuckel?"

"Fuckel?"

"The lawyer. My agent. That obnoxious crippled cock that's been crawling up your ass for the past month?"

"I reckon he'll be here in a little while. This is usually his first stop. You still haven't seen him?"

"No, but I want to see him now. Can you bring him here?"

Steve smiled as though everything was finally getting back to normal. He left and, within what seemed to be only minutes, he was back with Finkel.

I had to smile when I saw Finkel for the first time in almost a year. I could never tell how old he was, as he had been stricken with polio as a young boy. This left him without much of a knee in one leg, rendering it useless, but he still walked, limping along as he did, and he still talked very loud because he was all but deaf, too. I admired the ornery little fucker. He took me on when no one else had the balls. Maybe he needed me as much as I needed him, but it didn't matter, he was an irritating inspiration – all four feet of him.

"How's my boy doing?" he asked as he wobbled toward me. He looked at Lauren somewhat befuddled. "Who the fuck's she?"

"Lower your voice for crying out loud. She's sleeping."

"Sorry," he attempted to whisper. "Is she the one who made you crazy?"

"No. You are."

It occurred to me that Finkel was unable to speak at a normal volume. It was either naturally loud or an uncomfortable whisper. I made him whisper.

He sat in a chair next to my bed. His breathing was heavy. It was difficult for him to get around, but he did it. He looked at the box holding the manuscript.

"Is that it?" He reached for the box, and I slapped him in the forehead with back of my hand.

"What the fuck are you doing?" I asked.

"I want to see it. Fuck, Miles, I got the whole world up my ass."

"Really? The whole time I thought it was the polio."

Finkel's complexion had darkened. Being away from the shadows of the buildings in his normal Chicago-New York criss-cross had done him some good. He seemed a bit more relaxed, too. Maybe some of the lazy lay of the south had soaked in.

"The doctor says you're gonna croak."

"You should've been a poet, Finkel."

"Why didn't you let me know what was going on? I could've helped you, damnit."

"Have you caught any fish?"

"Ahh... I tried, but I keep losing them."

"What do you mean?"

"The line breaks or something. The cork goes under, I yank the stick, start to reel-in, and then the fucker's gone. No hook. No fish. No nothing."

"Give me your tie."

Finkel gave me his tie without an argument. It was the manuscript beneath my arm – as long as I had it, he'd give me his soul.

"I'm only gonna do this once so pay close attention."

I took the tie and looped it through my fingers. As I twisted the tie into a knot, Finkel watched like a curious child. I finished and tossed it back to him.

"Your knots aren't holding. Try this. It should solve the problem."

He held it up and looked at it as though he had found the final piece of the puzzle. He grinned and his heavy breathing grew worse. It was almost a whistle. I wished it was.

"Slow it down over there," I said. "You're gonna suck all the oxygen right out of this room and cheat me out of the time I have left."

"Thanks, Miles."

"Give me a piece of your letterhead and a black pen."

The pen and paper were in my hand within seconds. As Finkel played with his tie, I wrote down instructions. A bit disoriented from the morphine, I looked over the words, then handed the pen and paper to Finkel.

"Sign this."

He took the paper and read it. The knotted tie fell to the floor.

"You're out of your fucking mind!"

"Sign it. Then go find a copy machine around here, make a copy for yourself and bring me back the original."

"You don't know what you're doing, Miles. Why don't you think about it?"

"I have. You have five minutes."

"Miles, I can't let you do this."

"Fuck you. Four minutes."

"Miles!"

"I'd get to hobblin if I were you."

I saw the defeat flower in his eyes, but he got to hobbling and was back in a few minutes. Finkel was a man after money, but I couldn't blame him. What else could he do? Life had dealt him a shitty hand, and people, when they saw him, were afraid of him. He had to live in a world that would never allow him to feel as if it were his world, too. I despised the injustice, but it was useless to hate. I liked him with a tan. I liked imagining him sitting on the dock of his rented bay house with a fishing pole in his hand. He'd start with a cane pole, frozen shrimp and styrofoam cork. And after his first speckled trout he'd find a place in the world that was his only. Then, he'd be on his way.

Finkel gave me back the signed original. I gave him the manuscript.

"I don't know what to say, Miles."

"Goodbye would be best."

We shook hands, and he walked away. At the door, he turned back to me.

"What am I supposed to do with a kayak?"

"Live," I said.

He smiled and limped crookedly behind the close of the door. I never saw Finkel again.

lauren

It was Sunday. There would be no doctor visits, no visits of any kind. Sheri, the nurse I had screamed at when I came back to life, wouldn't come unless I called. I wouldn't call. Let her chain smoke, eat ding-dongs and watch sitcom reruns.

I had plugged the morphine line because I needed my mind. I wanted to talk to Lauren. I had to make a difficult decision. In retrospect, it was just as simple as all the others.

We lay naked in my bed. I had touched no softer skin than hers. She was amazing to me. To hold her in my arms meant everything. Faith had given me the strength to be somewhat selfless and the weakness to be completely exposed without apprehension. But Lauren had once been my only place in life. She was the closest I ever felt to home, anywhere on earth.

I had everything to gain and everything to lose. I knew that if I lay there and let death take me away, I would have lost my chance. I didn't want to lie there. Four white walls encasing sickness and self pity is no place to die and no way to live.

My sense of smell had returned and, with Lauren's head at rest on my chest, I could smell the mixture of aloe and fresh melons in her hair. I leaned in and breathed deeply, then kissed her. She looked up at me and smiled. Her smile was lovely, but I could see the fear of death behind it, and I had put it there.

"Did you love only me?"

"Miles, I could never love anyone but you."

"I want you to know that I'm leaving here soon."

"I know you are."

"You do?"

"Yes. And I want to be with you. I want to help you get through this. We'll go home and take care of things."

"I don't have a home, Lauren."

"I do."

"Chicago?"

"Of course, sweetie. We'll be together, and I can support us and take care of you. I know you think that you can't find inspiration there, but things have changed. I'm making money now. We can make this comfortable for you."

"Make what comfortable?"

"Your life, honey."

She meant my death. I could see myself tucked away in some cold corner of a beautiful old brownstone, neatly packed in with the others, just a block away from Lake Michigan, Michigan Avenue, the Chicago River. Just a block away from anywhere. The wood floors stained dark like maroon ice. The mahogany-paneled walls reaching up to clean, white ceilings. Snow gathered on the window sills. And on a bed of feather and cotton, I could look out at the city and watch the world breathe – smoke rising up past the glass, the condensation of people and machines perspiring lifeless air, killing the world without sympathy and checking watches from the inside of warm luxury cars as the tires of my hearse spit out the slush of dirt and snow rolling through the red lights and only one car following. He wasn't very well-liked. Maybe he outlived everyone he knew. That's sad. This is distracting me. I have a meeting. I'm about to piss all over myself. Soldier Field is waiting. It's five degrees on the sidewalk. Frozen spit. Petrified dog shit. Stoned out of my mind. So stoned I can only think of my wife and children murdered and bloody and cold. It's going to be a big check. Set for life. Poor bastard. All these people, and no one showed. Must have deserved it. We always get what we deserve. Who has money for new Christmas ornaments? Burn down the forest and sleep in. Bust my balls. A cold bottle of beer between my legs, and there's never enough. Lord, Jesus Christ, please have mercy on his soul. In the name of The Father, the Son, the Holy Spirit. If they'd have cremated him, I might have been on time for the national anthem. Time for a quick bump, compliments of the corpse. So that was it? Where are you now? In my way. That's all I know. Convicts get whatever people want them to have. The dying get whatever they want from people. And when the sun burns out, those people with solar panels on their roofs won't have time to be embarrassed. The sea will ice over a bed of discarded refrigerators. We won't decay anymore. Make homes out of the bodies. Do you want these saggy breasts pointing toward the street? A beautiful mantelpiece appointed with pale-blue penises. Everyone has cold feet. Obesity is gorgeous. The end has new meaning. Time is just a foursome of consonants and vowels. Bury that miserable bastard. Lock the cemetery gates. Melt the key. Let's go Bears!

"No mas pescado."

"What?"

"No mas pescado."

"Miles, what are you doing?"

"Pain is just a word, but sometimes so is morphine."

I released the drip on the morphine line. I had heard all that I needed to hear. I wanted to be pain free with Lauren for the next few hours. The decision was final. Now, I would float away on a morphine river and hold in my arms the only woman I would have died for. As I drifted away, she told me

I had pretty blue eyes. I loved her like no one else in life, but by daylight, everything would be different. She would receive what she truly wanted, her freedom from me.

west

At sunrise, I had made it halfway across Texas. Parked
behind a gas station in Junction, I watched the sun climb over
the rolling hill country. The morning air blew cold and dry.
It would become more of the same as I headed west. As for
water, the ocean was now only a memory.

I had to stop. The Jeep was running on fumes, and so was I.
It had been quite some time since I'd had solid food. This I
hadn't realized until the scent of warm baked bread tossed
about in the shifting breeze and told me fresh food was just
inside.

I sat as still as possible, but, no matter how much heat rose up
from the floorboard, I still shivered. The soft top for the Jeep
was too taxing for me to assemble so I didn't even try. Sit
still. A deer in the crosshairs. Lincoln in marble. Just
breathe. Just be. Just let what's left find the strength to
strengthen itself. The shivering decreased, coming only in
unwelcome, erratic spurts, but I felt it was enough to interact
with people and not bring unwanted attention to myself.

I pulled around to the gas pumps, shut off the engine and
stepped onto the pavement. My body wrenched, screaming at
me to be still. Ignore it. Pump the fucking gas and go inside.
I did.

The front door was no more than ten paces away. It might as
well have been a thousand miles. I smiled as I made my way
inside. Bukowski had said something similar about trying to
suck his own dick. He was a damn good man.

"Oh Lord, honey, ju must be freee-sing!"

She was a middle-aged Mexican woman standing behind the
counter. Her voice accentuated by both a border Spanish
vernacular and a Texas drawl. I could tell she was a product

of both sides of the border. I was wearing shorts, flip-flops and a T-shirt. I shivered as I walked inside.

"I didn't realize it was going to be so cold today."

"Oh, honey, we just gotta a big front in last night. It's espposed to be below freezin for thee rest of thee week. Don't ju have a coat or nothin?"

"Not with me."

"Well, we just got all our hunting gear out if jou'd like to look around."

"Do you have a lost and found box or something?"

"Did ju lose something?"

She asked as if I'd been there for an eternity. It pissed me off because I knew her husband and boyfriend and children and grandchildren, sisters and brothers and cousins and anyone close enough were the recipients of the contents of that box.

"Never mind."

There was no loss. Even though it hurt, there was no loss.

I turned and looked at the inside of the store. An orgy of colors stunned me, sickened me, but it was better than four white walls and five empty beds. This place had everything: a kitchen open twenty-four hours, a small restaurant, a deli with fresh cuts of meat, smoked sausage and jerky. There was beer and wine, rock candy and fountain sodas, ice cream, shampoo, cigarettes, doughnuts, kolaches, cheese, rubbers and clothes – camouflage hunting clothes.

A sign by the food counter spelled out the day's special. "Chicken-Fried Steak, Mashed Potatoes & Gravy, Blackeyed Peas & Peach Cobbler with Blue Bell Vanilla Ice Cream."

"Mam, may I have the special please?"

"Sure, honey. What ju want to drink?"

"Uh, coffee." Fuck that. I wanted a beer. Man, did I want a beer.

"Coffee's right there, hun, help jurself."

"Thank you."

How long had it been since I'd had a cup of coffee? At least ten years. I had stopped in Alexandria, Louisiana, on my way home from a trout slaughter with Grady O. We fished hard and drank harder for four days in a hidden bay fed fresh by the mighty Mississippi. We fished in pouring rain. We fished in sweat-soaked, sunny afternoon hours, in swarms of mosquitoes, in flat-bottom boats with gators lurking at our feet cooling in the water.

Cajuns like Grady O. love their beer, and they don't like folks who can't keep up. They don't like bitching either. Louie had doused himself in mosquito repellent until he smelled like an abandoned medicine cabinet. Grady O. and those other boys from the swamps eyed him as if they were watching a cold bath of blue blood splash and spill on their soil – desecrating it, pissing on it, telling them something's wrong with their home. He was ruined.

I took to drinking with Grady O. and never looked back. We built fires at night, cooked specs and boiled crawfish and red potatoes and corn on the cob. I might have had six hours of sleep throughout the ten day trip and, rolling through the asphalt pipeline of Pine, it caught up with me. Louie had flown home from Baton Rouge. Louie's pussy was really aching on that trip. It just wasn't for him. Anyway, I stopped at the only open gas station in sight, poured myself a large cup of coffee, added cream and all the sugar. I drank half the coffee. It was terrible. Old. Stale. Cold. Fuck it. I pulled to the side of the highway and poured the coffee in the grass. It was morning when the Louisiana Highway Patrol woke me, searched me, fucked with me, then sent my sorry ass back to Texas.

As I pulled a cup from the stack, I noticed the white cloth bandage that covered the heplock in my hand was coming loose. The intake for the intravenous line was almost completely exposed. Over my shoulder, no one seemed to notice. I wrapped it tighter, and poured myself a cup of coffee, added sugar and picked out a pair of insulated, camouflage overalls. I found an insulated hat of the same design with built-in earmuffs that flipped down if needed. The coffee was warm in my hand. I needed gloves. Only one pair fit. Extra-large bow-hunting gloves. They were thin and comfortable. There was a slit sewn in the bottom side of both the thumb and the index finger. The slits allowed the hunter to grip his bow tight without completely removing the glove. This was perfect for me. Where I was going, I'd definitely be the only one gripping my bow so I wanted it to be firm.

I slipped into the overalls and zipped them up. What a great fit. And pockets everywhere. Outside. Inside. Front. Back. Chest. Legs. Pockets I wanted to put to use immediately.

As I entered the men's room, the stench of fresh hot shit overwhelmed me. "Hellfire! Somebody call an ambulance!"

"Sorry, bubba," came a deep voice from behind a stall door. "I don't like it anymore an you do. Don't order today's special, whatever you do."

He flushed as a courtesy to me but it didn't matter. I poured my coffee down the sink and threw the cup away then vomited coffee and blood and bile into the garbage can. It felt as though my abdomen had split wide open, staples landing on the tile floor. I checked my incision, every staple was still intact. I rinsed my face and hair. From the pocket of my shorts, I retrieved a wad of cash. Ten thousand dollars.

One hundred one hundred dollar bills. It was all the money I had left. I had snatched it in the middle of the night from my apartment along with my uniform and my can of pills. I divvied the money into smaller amounts between one and two thousand, stuffed the cash into the assorted pockets of my new costume, then put five hundred in the money pocket of my shorts – left nut pocket. Take my last dollar, and you'll have to take my balls with it. Ask for it, and it's yours.

When I came out of the restroom, I looked like shrubbery in flip-flops. The whole ordeal had exhausted me. I sat down at a booth in the restaurant area and laid all the price tags from my new get-up on the table. Through the window, I saw an older looking man walking around my Jeep. There were lots of folks who just like to look at Jeeps. Enthusiasts. Freaks. Wannabes. Weirdoes. I was used to it, but this man was weathered, a drifter with a time-beaten bag of shit over his shoulder. I watched him closely as Old Faithful was sticking out the back and the morphine bag that I had taken from the infirmary was wrapped in a towel beneath the seat. He could have Old Faithful but not the morphine, not now. Priorities had changed.

"Here ju are, sweetie." She put a food plate of such proportions before me that I was lost in its aroma, its warmth, its color. "Can I get ju anything else?"

"Do yall sell suppositories?"

"I'm sorry?"

"No need. Suppositories? Silver bullets? Medicine for hemorrhoids?"

"Ju got hemorrhoids, too? Oh dear."

"I believe so. It's my first time."

"Honey, ju're just a mess, aren't ju? What'd ju do to your hand?"

"What's your name?" I reached and gently touched her shoulder with my clean hand, tucking the heplocked hand beneath the table.

"Maria."

"Maria. The name of my very first love. The Mother of God Hisself." Maria looked confused so I smiled innocently at her to let her know I was speaking of two different women, though it was really delirium attacking a feeble, dying body. "Maria, did you know that some folks think Jesus Christ was just the bastard son of an illegitimate conception?"

"Are ju one of them real religious persons?"

"No. I don't believe in religion."

"How can ju not believe in somethin that already exists?"

"Who says it exists?"

"Well, I do for one."

"Why?"

"I'm a Catholic."

"You look like a human to me."

In the corner of my eye, I noticed the drifter outside had taken the relaxed position of leaning against my Jeep. An older man. Dark red leather faced. White hair. White beard. His hair tied in a pony tail with a wide dirty bandana.

"Maria, do you know who that man is out there?"

"Him? He is just a bum."

"A bum?"

"Jes. He's been here all dis morning trying to catch a ride."

"Where's he going?"

"He says California, but I don't think he really cares. I'm sure he just wants money."

I took up the tags from my new clothes and handed them to Maria, requesting a check for the gas, clothes and food. She smiled and walked away. "Maria?" I called. "Would you please bring me an empty plate?"

"Sure, Senor."

She sat the plate and the check on the table. I had worked-up a two hundred twenty-two dollar tab. From my nut pocket I counted four hundred dollars and gave it to her. She went to register and returned with my change – seventy-eight dollars. She had either decided to tip herself a hundred dollars or simply miscounted. To miss by one hundred dollars was possible, but highly improbable. A witch in clerk's clothing. He just wants money. He just wants fucking money. Those fucking bums.

I tapped on the window trying to get the attention of the man leaning on my vehicle. He wouldn't look my way. I knocked harder on the glass. He peered in at me, and I motioned for him to come in.

As he came through the door, I noticed that Maria would not look at him – neither would anyone else. He was one from whom the world chose to turn away. I waved him over to me and gestured for him to sit down. He took a seat opposite me in the booth, setting his old bag on his lap. At close range, I could sense that he was much younger than his unkempt cover revealed. His eyes were like two crystallized drops of Caribbean water – blue, tranquil and without fear. His face, his eyes, his cheeks, his hands wrinkled with sea wear. He was probably no older than me. My age. Strange. It suddenly occurred to me that I would turn thirty-three the next day.

I took half of everything from my plate, put it on the empty plate and pushed it in front of him. He started eating without a word. I watched him for a moment –then ate my first bite of solid food in weeks.

"You know how to drive?" I asked.

"I know how to drive."

"Well, how boutcha."

"Better than you."

"What's your name?"

"James Jonas."

"You wantin to go in any particular direction?"

"I'm trying to get back to the ocean."

"Which one?"

"Pacific."

I pushed my plate toward him and offered my portion. I felt suddenly immersed in ice water. My throat swelled, my hands and feet burned frozen. My body was calling out, and I was without choice but to listen. In the handicap stall of the men's room, I lay on the floor exhaustedly finding comfort in the stick and stench of humanity's disregard for itself. On my knees I vomited green bile, blood and the little food I had eaten. Back to the floor I thought of soldiers dying from horrific wounds in combat. Young men on foreign soil, their legs lying twenty yards away, their state of shock easing the pain, but the face of death looking them in the eye. What does it mean to be dead? Are there feelings involved? Could the mind function for a time in another capacity when the body is nothing but lifeless tissue?

Someone entered the restroom. I pulled myself off the floor and sat on the commode. I tried to catch my breath, to find stillness, to let my body gather. I sat in stillness until I felt I had the strength to move. I needed to leave. I needed to get out of there. I was uncertain if the sheriff's office would waste their time and money chasing a dead man, but I was certain that it was a possibility. Small towns in Texas don't get fucked over.

At the sink, I cleansed my face with warm water. I was pale, thin and looked much the part of death standing. In the mirror was a life that had brought to me many things, all of which were soon to be forgotten but not without consequence. As I looked into my eyes, I knew that death could not be evaded, but I also knew I was still breathing. I was living. I was alive, and I intended to keep living, stay alive, live until life tore itself away from me bleeding and fighting for anything left. I wouldn't have had it any other way.

I walked out and motioned for James Jonas to come with me. At the Jeep, I gave him the keys and told him to go west. He did. We did. And the heat blowing on my bare feet was like the warmth of a beautiful woman in my bed.

On the road, I reinserted the morphine line into my hand and tied the bag to the roll bar with a piece of fishing line. James Jonas watched but said nothing. As I began to fade, I asked him to drive to Fort Stockton. I said we'd have dinner there, spend the night and go north in the morning. I told him that I had always heard that Montana was beautiful. He said it was.

I asked if he had a driver's license, but was out before he answered.

...

It was dusk by the time we reached the motel in Fort Stockton. I woke at the touch of James Jonas tugging at the line in my hand. I pulled my hand away.

"What the fuck are you doing?" I asked.

"We're here."

"Where?"

"Fort Stockton. The room's forty-five for the both of us or we can get two for thirty-nine each. Either way, I only have fifteen dollars."

"You want money?"

"No, but the woman behind the register does." He smiled at me. "I thought I'd go in and pay, then help you get inside. If you're uncomfortable with me in the room, I'll sleep in the Jeep, if it's all right with you."

I cut off the drip in the morphine line and pulled it from my hand. From my nut pocket I gave him the hundred dollar bill and waited until he returned with the room keys.

We pulled around to the back of the motel and parked close to the door. James Jonas went inside and turned on the lights and the heater. As I climbed my way out of the seat, I fell and hit my head hard on the pavement. It was an hour or so later when I woke. I was in bed. The morphine bag hung from a hanger across the room and Old Faithful stood tall in the corner by the door. James Jonas sat in a chair next to me. He held a bag of ice to my head.

"You took a pretty good spill," he said. "If it hadn't knocked you out, I'd still be laughing."

"Are you hungry?" I asked.

"It doesn't matter to me."

"Do you like yard bird?"

"Yeah, I like it fried."

"How bout you run get us a bucket. I could handle some deep fried epidermis."

"I ain't so sure it's a good time for you to be alone."

"I'm never alone." I looked him in the eye just as Piggy had looked at me that evening on the boat. "I will never be alone."

"I know, but I was thinking that you might doze off if I leave you here alone. You're supposed to stay awake after a fall like that."

"I'm awake. I'll be fine. Just turn the television on real loud and keep all the lights on. If I fall asleep this bag of ice will land on my balls. If that doesn't wake me up, then I ain't supposed to wake up."

"You want anything else besides chicken and potatoes?"

"Beer."

"Any particular flavor?"

"Cold. Texas."

"Right back."

James Jonas walked out the door, and I closed my eyes. I thought of the need to stay awake. It was as though I dreamed the thoughts. Whatever was on TV was where I went, but I only hovered from one ridiculous scene to the next. Then the bag of ice fell into my lap, and I was awake, again. I sat on the edge of the bed so I would be forced to hold myself up. It helped, but I wanted to slip away again. Fly through TV land, fantasy land, the land of degradation. I fought it off for quite some time, but it was just too much, and darkness came over me. The bag of ice fell to the floor. In a heavy fog of thought and confusion, I found myself finally nearing home.

...

The house was old. It was home to me and a few critters and crawlers. The air was a bit cooler at night due to a climb of ten thousand feet above sea level. Sea level. That was funny. There was not a sea within a thousand miles in any direction of this place – and when has anything ever been level? The windows to the old house were all open and I heard the occasional siren mixed in with periodic traffic rolling by. The trains passed through during the day. They stormed through en route to some place other than where I was. At night, they also came, but I relaxed and let them reel through me and churn my dreams with their heavy roll.

"I haven't heard this much noise since I was last in New York City."

I was speaking to Lauren. She lay in bed next to me. Her mother was next to her, lying there like a sick seal, chain-smoking long menthol cigarettes, coughing and bitching about something awry in her miserable life.

I rose at the feel of another's presence in the house. "Don't get up, honey. Come back and lie down next to me and mama." Lauren held up the old Indian blanket and patted softly on the mattress. "You can sleep inside me. You love to sleep that way."

I heard the menthol snort of the dying seal.

"I have to piss," I said and moved down the hallway. In the darkness, I saw the back of a man's head leaning against the window. He was sitting on the porch bench. Large dumbbells rose and fell with the flex of his wide, muscular neck. Immediately, I recognized him. It was my brother, Carl, passing the time with some late night exercise. "Hey. The door's open. Why didn't you just come in?"

"I didn't want to wake you."

"I was already awake. Lauren and her mother and I were in bed together." He looked crudely ill at my words and my return expression revealed my concurrence. "Come in. What brings you way up here?"

"I've got a tryout with the Seahawks in the morning. Did you know Mickey's inside? He was here when I got here."

I left the screen door open for my brother and walked toward the hallway that led to the bathroom, passing Mickey along the way. He stood behind the glass panes of an old red phone booth. We saw one another peripherally, but I said nothing to him. Mickey was doing what he did best – fucking over someone on the phone. Someone was going to get fucked and it wouldn't be my cousin. It never had been, even through all the years before I fell away from their realities – the family. Things changed. And I never knew why.

At the doorway of the bathroom, I noticed Sammy, a childhood friend, seated on the toilet immersed in the sports page. It had been twenty-five years since I'd last seen that piece of shit. And to think I actually caught someone truly being himself – this was an odd blessing, a gift of holy proportion, a man being nothing more than what he was. We said nothing. It would have been pointless. He was drowning in statistics, and only the final number could save him.

Back to the porch. Mickey was no longer on the phone. The red phone booth was no longer. Outside were a number of people stirring about on the driveway. I knew none of them. A man with a gray beard handed me a plastic bag of candies and pastries.

"Where's my brother?"

"The big, mean lookin fella? Don't say shit?"

"Yessir."

"He done gone inside."

Both his travel bag and dumbbells were gone.

I looked inside the plastic bag. "The brownies are fudge and hemp," said the bearded man.

I devoured two immediately, looking about at the strange faces milling about in the moonlight like the ghosts of dead cattle.

"There's white chocolate covered mushrooms and the small ones that look like Christmas cookies are Scooby Snacks sprinkled with cocaine dust."

I stuffed my mouth. "These are quite delicious."

"I made them myself. I was a baker in the Navy."

"Fascinating. But what in the fuck would a naval vessel need with a banker?"

"I said baker."

"My father was a baker."

I saw Mickey stirring in the yellow light beneath the carport talking to a few of the strangers. Each one held a plastic bag of goodies. Mickey held two in one hand – the other held a burning cigarette. I reached for another Scooby Snack and asked the bearded man what each bag went for. "Three hundred." I bit the snack in half, swallowed, then put the other half back inside the bag.

"Oh, fuck it."

I grabbed the other half and swallowed it down.

I began to wonder: Who did I know here? I had no money. My last five dollars had gone for Lauren's mother's menthols earlier that day. I sensed that I was expected to pay because it was my house. So I looked around for one of my rich friends but found none. As I walked inside the house, Mickey avoided my look. Fuck him. Fuck em all. I locked the door behind me.

In the bathroom, Sammy still dwelled on the commode – he had several more pages to go. Three other guys were standing at the sink mirror, picking at their teeth and drinking beer. Two of them were my wealthy friends from Tennessee. The other appeared to be of some relation to Sammy – a sidekick, a boyfriend, a freeloader, a man in need of a toilet.

"We're going home, honey," Lauren said as she passed by the doorway, "It looks like you might need the space."

"No. I want you to stay." I looked over at her mother, *"You're welcome to leave though. There's a cemetery up the highway. You might ought to get an early start."* Lauren told me she loved me but was leaving because her mother didn't feel welcome.

"Good, because she's not."

At the bathroom sink, Will, an old high school friend and trust fund baby sighed at me with disgust at the sight of Lauren's mother. "No wonder you keep it so dark in here, Miles."

"Where's my brother?"

"Upstairs. Asleep." Sammy spoke for the first time, but did not look away from the paper. *"He said that if we made too much noise he'd kill all of us."*

In the kitchen, I drank cold water from a plastic cup. It was life cold and clean and holy.

Shutting the door to my bedroom, I dropped my shorts to the floor and tossed my t-shirt aside in the darkness. The sheets were cool and soft, but my dick was hot and hard. I scratched the thought of pissing in the garbage can and drifted to sleep thinking of how nice it would've been if Sammy hadn't found the sports page.

...

It was an ice-cold rag that brought me back. James Jonas held it to my forehead and shook me by the shoulder until I looked him in the eye. I smelled chicken and biscuits.

"Did you get the taters?"

"Yes. Would you like some?"

"In a minute."

He held a cold soda to my mouth and suggested that I drink as much of it as I could. He said the sugar would give me energy.

"Are you a doctor?"

"No. I'm a bum."

"Me too."

I sucked on the soda, and it was delicious. James Jonas pulled a small table between the beds and spread out a feast of fried chicken, biscuits, red beans and rice, mashed potatoes and brown gravy. He set a cold bottle of Lone Star beer in front of me. It wasn't fish and scotch, but it wasn't a feeding tube either.

Just as he had in Junction, James Jonas ate without a word. I peeled the skin from a chicken breast and smelled it, then chewed it slowly and swallowed it. It was spicy and greasy and lit up my taste buds, which had been asleep for too long. I tore some white meat from the bone and savored the taste. It was juicy and tender. When it was time to swallow, I swallowed. And, for a moment, I sat in wonder.

"Inhale deep and slow through your nose, then exhale just as slow through your mouth. That'll help."

James Jonas didn't look at me when he spoke. He just kept eating.

I heeded his advice as I ate the mashed potatoes. It worked well. The nausea was minor. I came close, but I did not vomit. After several minutes, I sat back in bed, twisted the cap off the beer and closed my eyes.

"You're not gonna fall asleep are ya?"

"Not with a full beer in my hand. That'd be a sin."

"Are you a sinner?"

"I grew up being told I was."

"Catholic?"

"Yeah," I said. "You?"

"Guilty."

"Are you a sinner?" I asked.

"I guess that depends on who you ask. Ask a priest. Ask God. Most likely you'll get two different answers."

"I'm asking you."

"I don't lie. I don't cheat. And I don't steal. This may disqualify me as a sinner."

"I believe you're right."

"When did you experience your epiphany?"

"A couple days ago in jail."

James Jonas didn't inquire as to why I had been in jail. Nor did he ask about the scars on my face. He didn't inquire into much of anything. This told me many things about him. I liked him.

The long hours on the road had taken their toll. I closed my eyes and sipped my beer. James Jonas asked if the beer was good. I opened my eyes and looked at him. "It's spectacular."

I set the beer on the night table and closed my eyes. Within a few minutes, he said something. I couldn't make it out. I asked him what he had said.

"Nothing."

This happened many times over the next few hours. As I rested and gathered my thoughts, I realized he was trying to keep me from falling asleep. I let him do it because I didn't want to die in a cheap motel room with a half empty bottle of beer. I wouldn't allow such soft bones in my heaven.

At four in the morning, James Jonas woke me. Every light in the room was on. He asked if I wanted another beer. I said no – then I said yes. Instead of giving me a beer, he thanked me for the meals that we'd had together. He thanked me for the ride. He thanked me for the motel room. He thanked me for very little things.

"What's in California?" I asked.

"My daughter."

"Does she know you're coming?"

"She don't know who I am."

"You aim to change that, I reckon?"

"I aim to change that forever."

He meant what he said. I didn't know the man well, but I knew when a man's heart was pure, and I was happy for him.

"I think you're okay to sleep now. I'll wake you at dawn."

I reached for my beer, but it was empty. My mind was empty, too. I slept without a thought.

bye james jonas

When we left the motel I asked James Jonas to take me
through town, through the old neighborhoods, the main street,
the oil company parking lots. We weren't in the car for two
minutes when I saw it – a 1976 International Harvester Scout
II. It sat in a used car lot that held no more than a dozen other
vehicles.

"Pull in here, James Jonas."

He turned in, and I directed him to the Scout. The paint was
dark green, old and fading. The tires were no less than new.
There were two spares in the rear compartment. The interior
was blue cloth. It had four-wheel drive, automatic
transmission, air conditioning, heat, a removable hard top and
a soft top in the back seat.

A heavyset gentleman named Poochie came out and asked me
how I was. Being in my new uniform, I told him that my feet
were cold, but otherwise things were just as fine as sunshine.
Poochie wore a Mexican straw cowboy hat, a heavily
starched white shirt with his name embroidered over the left
pocket and a pair of tight fitting polyester brown slacks
strapped to his big belly with an even bigger belt buckle.

"How boutcha?"

"How you boys doin?"

"We're both completely fucked-up, but I like this here
vehicle."

"Well it's a goodun. Everthin's original except the engine.
The previous owner put a brand new V-8 in about ten
thousand miles ago. Would ya like to take her fer a spin?"

"What you want for it?"

"Five and a half."

"If that price is negotiable I'd like to drive it."

"I'll get the keys."

Poochie went inside his office trailer. The air conditioner hummed from a small window around the side. James Jonas asked if I'd minded if he took the Jeep down the street. There was a thrift store he wanted to visit.

"Can you be back in thirty minutes?"

"Thirty minutes."

He drove away.

Poochie came out with the keys. The Scout fired right up and I drove it down the street to the first stop light, turned around and parked it where I had found it.

Inside the office trailer I offered Poochie four thousand dollars cash. He said he couldn't accept it. There were just too many folks interested in it.

"I'm not interested – I'm offering."

He apologized and so did I. Then I went outside and waited on James Jonas. It wasn't more than a minute when Poochie came out and asked if I'd meet him half way.

"Poochie, I'd meet you half way if I could, but I can't. I'm sure one of them other folks will come through for you."

"You said cash earlier. Did you mean cash cash?"

I unzipped my inside chest pocket and showed him forty one-hundred dollar bills. He nodded me back inside.

I signed a bunch of papers that I didn't read, shook Poochie's hand and drove the Scout to the thrift store where the Jeep was parked outside. I took the bag of morphine, my can of pills and a lighter and put them inside the Scout. From my wallet, I unfolded the title to the Jeep and signed it over to James Jonas.

I stood outside and looked up at the sky. It was a sky like I had never before seen – endless, cloudless, clean, pure and forever, but without any water to glorify it. It didn't need it. It was its own sky. And in that moment, there was no pain. It was there, but I was outside it. I knew then that my journey was real.

"Here ya go."

James Jonas handed me several plastic shopping bags.

"You'll need these where you're goin." In the bags were used blue jeans, shirts, socks, a canvas jacket and a pair of well-worn bull hide cowboy boots. "Hold on, there's one more thing inside."

He went into the store and came back out holding a beautiful felt cowboy hat. It was gray, weathered with years of dirt and wind and hard living. He placed it on my head. It was a perfect fit.

"How'd you know where I was going?"

"You talk in your sleep."

"I do?"

"You did."

"I don't remember dreaming."

"People who live dreams have no need to remember them."

"You ought to know," I said. "Thank you, James Jonas. Thank you for everything."

I opened the door to the Scout, shed my camouflage overalls, my shorts, my flip-flops and my shirt. I tossed all of it into the passenger seat and stood naked in the parking lot digging through the bags of clothes. James Jonas said nothing about the track of staples. I slipped into the jeans, put on the shirt and snapped the buttons. As I slid the socks over my feet, I realized that this was the first time I had worn socks in years. The boots were more comfortable than the socks. I donned my new hat and looked at James Jonas. He laughed, and I laughed with him.

"This is amazing. How'd you know my numbers?"

"I made law enforcement uniforms in prison."

I handed him the keys to the Jeep. "Have a safe journey. The rod and reel's name is Old Faithful. Treat the old gal right and she'll bring you lots of bread and beauty." I gave him the title. He unfolded it and read it.

"I can't, Miles."

"I'm sorry. You must. Anyway, how in the fuck am I supposed to drive two vehicles at the same time? Besides, a man with more than one key is no longer just a man, he's a slave."

He put the title in his pocket and held the key tight in his hand.

"You might want to stay off the main highways for a while – just in case. You understand, of course, James Jonas?"

"Can I ask a favor of you, Miles?"

"You wanna see my dick again?"

"Not particularly."

He reached into his old travel bag and retrieved a tethered copy of *Shredded Thoughts*.

"Sign it for me?"

I did. He thanked me and put the book back in his bag.

"Will you write again?"

"No. Never again." He kept looking at me. "Well, I might jot down a few things. One never knows."

He nodded at me as if to tell me that that was what I needed to tell him.

We shook hands and wished one another fruitful journeys. He drove away with Old Faithful's watermelon lure glimmering in the sunshine. I looked at my reflection on the glass door of the thrift store. Change, I thought, is a funny thing. I never saw James Jonas again. And I looked like a complete ass in that hat.

el rancho

As I drove south down Highway 67, the sky grew bigger by the mile. I passed through the town of Alpine and bought a bottle of scotch. It was one of two bottles on the shelf and almost twice the price you'd pay in a big city. From Alpine, I drove twenty-five miles west to the town of Marfa. I had hoped to make it there before five in order to meet the real estate agent. I made it to his office at four-thirty, but he was already gone.

Across the street was the Paisano Hotel, famous for housing the actors and crew of the great Texas movie *Giant*: James Dean, Elizabeth Taylor, Rock Hudson. Over the years, the hotel had changed hands several times. Each time, there were different plans for the place. A couple from Houston had finally purchased it and had made the wise decision to renovate it, but still hold on to its heritage. It was a beautiful old building with a large courtyard in front, a grand fountain with flowing water, upstairs balconies, an indoor pool and the flags of America, Texas and Mexico hanging softly over the courtyard.

Since it was the middle of the week, I was able to get a suite with a balcony overlooking the courtyard. The downside was that the room was upstairs. The other downside was that there was no elevator. I stood at the foot of the staircase and tried to appear as if I were just enjoying the old Texas ambiance, which I was, but I was also wondering if I could make it to the top without dying.

"Fuck it!" I said.

"I'm sorry?" The girl asked from behind the counter.

"Fuck it. I just said fuck it."

"Yes sir."

With both hands on the rail, I pulled myself up the stairs, down the hallway, opened the door to my suite, closed it and fell to my knees in agony. Turning to my side, I covered my face with my hands and cried like a man tortured in war time. When I could take it no longer, my body let me know. The lights inside went dark, and I was out.

...

I was fortunate that I had turned sideways before I fainted. The bloody mess that I vomited stained only my shirt and not the carpet. In the mirror, I was something from the grave – sickly thin, blood drizzles dried on my face, my throat and neck, my hair. My eyes were no longer blue as Lauren had said. They were the eyes of a lame beaten wolf. Gray. Silver. Pewter. Red. Cadaverous. Dead. Living on borrowed, no, not borrowed, stolen time. Who would I have given it back to?

In the shower, I sat on the tiled floor and let the hot water wash away my shivering. With a soapy rag, I scrubbed the incision and picked away the green ooze that had dried between the staples. Pain had become more than just a word, and only the water and steam kept me from screaming out my death song to the world.

In the bedroom, I poured scotch into a glass and set it next to my can of pills on the nightstand. I tied the morphine bag to the headboard, plugged the line into the heplock. I could see an infection growing in my hand. I swallowed a handful of pain killers with neat single malt and turned on the television. The French doors that led to the balcony were open, and the breeze was cool and dry and comfortable. There was no air conditioning. It was useless in the high desert. There would be no more humidity. No more wet morning grass. No more grass.

As the drugs began to take effect, my eyes grew heavy. I fought the heaviness with another mouthful of scotch, trying to focus on the History Channel's story of Charles Manson and his gang. I drifted as they showed a re-enactment of the night Sharon Tate and others were slaughtered in Roman Polanski's home. I slowed the drip just enough for some comfort and finished what was left in my scotch glass. What was wrong with these fucks? Kids so lost they'd hold on to anything that made them feel the world needed them. And Charles – intelligence so misdirected it would change the mindset of America. The power of persuasion. It's as strong as the raging ocean. Why some California lifer hadn't choked that coward to death I didn't know. Maybe Chuck had gotten even better.

My naked body lay just beneath my line of sight. My ribs showed plain as day. My skin just a thin pane of bone and vein. It was a depressing sight, like a child starving in a land far from that comfortable bed. I covered my body with a white cotton sheet and fell away into the fog of insanity and slept with my mind racing in bloody history.

It was dark outside when I woke. Immediately I disconnected the morphine line. The bag was near empty. I had fallen asleep with the French doors that led to the balcony open. The temperature had plummeted some thirty degrees after the sun had gone down. My suite was extremely cold. I shook in uncontrollable fits. Cold weather was something I was not used to. My days had always been hot, scorching hot. And my nights the same.

I sat upright and planted my bare feet on the floor to help stop the spin. Wrapped in the down comforter, I stepped out onto the balcony and looked over the railing. There were tourists sitting at the outdoor tables eating dinner. Some asshole yelled "Take it off!" So I did. I spread my arms wide, exposing myself to the strangers. His laughing subsided, and he didn't look at me again. Maybe it was the freshly cut scar or the half hard cock, but something really brought a downer to the party. There's always one of these guys around. No matter how far you go. Life of the party, huh? Where's your fucking lamp shade? That was enough of that dickhead. I went back into my room and shut the doors behind me.

Facing the dresser, I poured myself another scotch and swallowed it down. There was a mirror over the dresser. It was old with beveled glass. In it stood my only truth, and I was forced to face it.

It was strange to come to the realization that I had, in a way, committed suicide. In my deliberate ignorance, my disease had always been excused away as something that I had eaten or a nagging virus that I just couldn't kick. And there had always been the hangover excuse. But after so much time of battling unrelenting bloody bouts with my guts, the diagnosis was what I hoped it never would be.

"You're dying from cancer."

I said this to my withered reflection in the mirror before climbing back into bed. All my past procrastination and foolish pride had expedited my impending death, allowing more spreading time for the tumors – and spread they did, like mushrooms after a southern summer rain.

I always knew I had no choice but to follow that which bestowed itself upon me, but I did have a few choices. They were just extenders of time – miserable time. I had no choice. I wasn't the one in charge – ever. But they finally proved to me what I had long known. "I'm dying," I said, lying back in bed. "I've always known that from the day I was born I was dying, but dying normally, aging to death, if you will."

I peeled the lid from my can of pills and milled around with my fingers. From the bottom of the can, I pulled a matchbox. I shook it, but it made no sound. Pushing the tray from the sleeve, I discovered a tightly compressed garden of Hawaiian weed. To me, it was like finding gold, flaming gold, gold so brilliant that it could pay my way to anywhere in the universe.

I tossed the comforter back on the bed and slipped into my camouflage overalls, grabbed the room key and stepped out into the hallway. I looked right, then left, then walked toward the stairwell that led down to the lobby. On the wall was a sign reading Ice & Vending Machines Downstairs. Fuck me.

I took one step down then stopped. Just down the hallway floor was a food tray waiting to be picked up. I went to it, grabbed an empty Coke can and returned to my room.

In the sink, hot water ran over the can. No telling who had their lips on that thing. Probably funny man down in the courtyard. I dried the can and made a makeshift pipe out of it, something I'd done a thousand times before.

After draining one more glass of scotch, I got in bed and smoked that red-headed bud until it was nothing but ash. It was delicious and warmed me. Pain had suddenly become just a word again. I shut off the light and watched the television. It was the same shit about Manson and Tex and all the girls Chuck had fucked in more ways than one. "Good luck in Hell," I said, and turned off the television.

"It's me God. I reckon I'm getting pulled out early. If that's my fault or Your calling or both or neither, so be it. If you can, I need just a bit more time. It's important. Otherwise I wouldn't bother You. So please, if You would, move me back a few spots in line. Fill my spot in with a murderer or a rapist or some other damned soul. Those fucks deserve the wrath that awaits them."

Some people pray nightly, as if chanting the same old hymns before falling asleep will secure their salvation. Some people pray when they have no other choice. Some don't pray at all. I was one of the latter. For the past year, I had thought incessantly. But when it was out of sheer desperation, I thought aloud – no matter when, no matter where. And this time was no different. I really didn't consider what I had said to God a prayer so much as a divine request. I was excited knowing that tonight I did not pray, but instead, in undivided selfishness, called out for something specific from God. It was similar to the feeling of awaiting the response from the bloody face in the dirt after finally punching the bully in the nose. To me, making deals with The Almighty was something one should never do, especially if one offers to do something to God's pleasing after He has fulfilled *His* end of the bargain. This type of transaction was beyond the realm of God, even insulting. Yet it was a perfect deal to make with the Devil: Do this for me now, and afterwards I'll make it up to you. I felt that selfishness was not part of God's vocabulary, but my clock was ticking faster every day. Just a few more ticks were all I needed. My rationale made me comfortable, and, quickly, I drifted off to sleep.

It was five-thirty a.m. In a field on the edge of town, I waited fretfully for the sun to come creeping over Paisano Pass and thaw out the chilly morning, spilling its hopeful light over the vast, mountainous majesty of West Texas. Normally I was sluggish and muddled in the morning, either tired or hung over or just plain sick, but this morning was different – I couldn't stand still, as if I were late jumping a ride on Pop's boat to spend another day wading in the murky waters of Mud Cut fighting reds. I paced about kicking up rocks from the dirt and repeatedly checking east to see how much color had gathered in the starlit sky. It was just anxiety, as I was eager to write about the dream I'd had that night after being so egotistical with God. I kept thinking of it, a sandy twister dancing and twirling about the mush of my mind, snatching every detail I possibly could, while I could.

The eastern skyline spewed a tiny hint of indigo over the horizon. It was coming, but agonizingly slow. I stayed because I knew since childhood that nothing I could ever write could be more beautiful than a West Texas sunrise.

141

As the sun broke Paisano Pass the black night faded away, taking with it all the stars, but leaving the moon behind. A brilliant scarlet glow filled the world, and the big sky grew as blue as the deepest ocean. Suddenly, I was standing still, completely captured by the overwhelming splendor of another day arriving.

"Thank you, God. That was *fucking* beautiful." After a moment of soaking in a touch of warm bliss, I drove back to the hotel, scaled the stairs like a cat after a mouse and entered my room.

Sitting down at the table in my room, I took a piece of hotel letterhead and scribbled the following:

The Only Dream I Have Ever Won –

At first, I heard the humming of a diesel engine growing louder as a big rig pulled into the parking lot. Then it drifted away, backing into the Best Western Motel across the highway. In reality, there was no Best Western across the highway. There was nothing across the highway except vast pastures stretching northwest toward the Davis Mountains, the Puertacitas and the sleeping Hay Stacks. I knew this for certain because I woke early and walked into the open fields to watch the sky burn in brilliant orange hues as the sun peaked the crests of the Twin Sisters in the Pass.

The hum of the truck's engine slowed to a purr. Then I heard a man on a microphone.

"Ladies and gentlemen, please give a warm West Texas welcome to Mr. Randy Quaid!"

As a waiting crowd roared, I wondered what was going on. It was four fucking o'clock in the morning! And Randy Quaid? He was an actor as far as I knew. Was he there to sing? Did he do standup comedy on the side? Was he just more famous in this part of Texas? At least it wasn't at this motel, I thought, and I was too tired to care anymore. Shortly thereafter, the door of my motel room opened and two young men entered, from my drowsy perspective just a couple of squabbling silhouettes. As I watched them and tried to make clear what they were arguing about, my typical one room double/double had grown into a large suite, complete with a full kitchen, a large living area and another bedroom. Deep in the darkness behind the two men entering, I lay in bed watching.

My scratchy voice sounded out from the darkness, "Excuse me, but what in the fuck are you doing in here?"

They turned toward me in sequence as I ended my question. Light broke the darkness as one of them flipped the switch in the living area.

"Who the fuck are you?" asked a short, stocky man with blonde, crew-cut hair and a faint, almost transparent moustache.

Had it not been for its excessive length, I might never have noticed it.

"This is our fucking room. Get your ass out."

Both men approached me rather quickly as I reached for my .45, holding it low alongside my bed, opposite their approach. Crewcut's sidekick, a young, brown-haired handsome fellow, brandished a knife. Actually it was a small, round-bladed hunting knife with a black rubber palm and finger-like grip.

"I'll just find out what the fuck's going on," I said, reaching for the phone. "Did you two dicks pick the lock to get in here?"

"Nobody's callin no one, partner!" barked Brownhair (herein referred to as Rob, as in Rob Lowe, the actor who gets into filming himself fornicating). Blondie brandished his own knife, a 12-inch long sword-like skinning knife.

"Hey!" I said to Blondie. "I have one just like that, but mine's only eight inches long, just a few shy of my dick, Bret."

I felt myself laughing in my sleep.

I pointed my gun at Rob's head. "I'm callin." At this point, he attacked and this is where this particular dream differed from all the others. I wasn't frozen or wedged or restricted or stuck in the mud. I was free to respond, to act and react. Suddenly I was fucking fearless and alive. Clint Eastwood spitting a syrupy wad of tobacco juice on a dusty saloon floor.

Up from my bed, a beautiful girl with long curly, black hair and perfect, natural breasts quickly joined in the fight against me. But she was no match. I snatched away Blondie's long skinning knife and with a perfect swing, left her beautiful lopped-off head rocking on the floor. Her body fell quietly somewhere into a place of expendable non-issue.

Rob came at me. I fired off six rapid rounds, each one missing by a mile. Oh shit, I thought, this is turning into one of those standard I'm-going-to-die-defenseless-and-shamed dreams.

From the living area, another woman entered. She was tall with pale skin and long fiery red hair, cut in a straight line just above the crack of her bare ass. She seemed so annoyed, as if Rob and Blondie were keeping her from getting ready as a woman would get ready.

"Can't you two idiots do anything right?"

144

The last bullet in my clip found a home dead center between the gleam of her sapphire eyes. Poor thing fell off into the darkness without a sound.

This situation had just become too much. I broke for the door and found myself in the hallway, naked and bulletless. Rob and Blondie (herein referred to as Bob Beamer) chased quickly behind. I ran down the empty motel halls, but never bothered pounding on doors for help. I wasn't even looking for a stairwell or any type of exit. I was just sort of enjoying running around naked with an unloaded pistol.

They stuck close behind me as I made my way back to my room. Storming inside with Rob and Bob Beamer still on my ass, to my surprise I found another beautiful woman standing calmly inside. Though faceless, her sandy-blonde hair was shoulder length, straight and copious, just the type I loved to run my fingers through. As I rushed past her, she drew a .38 caliber pistol, which I took from her with such ease it was as though she were handing it to me. Maybe she was. Turning to face her, I quickly buried a slug squarely in her very distinct, very sexy Adam's apple. She fell toward me and I heard no sounds of pain from her as she expired. My preoccupation was with Rob and Bob Beamer and myself, suddenly right back in our prior position.

I pointed the .38 at Rob as he waved his knife at me, telling me again and again to "...bring it on, mother fucker." Rob, being the daring bastard he was, attacked again. From less than a trio of feet I fired the .38 at his head. One. Two. Three. Four. Each slug still missing its target, but not by far. The bullets that blasted through the kitchen cabinets behind Rob's head were not lead, but rubber, and I distinctly remember their being a chalky, limey-yellow. Soaring citrine rubber missiles. Inaccurate, at best.

Why could I not kill this guy? I'd seen Rob Lowe movies before, maybe not by choice, but I had. The guy had probably fucked half the gals in Hollywood and he just didn't seem like that bad of a guy. Maybe if I'd gotten to know him, I might have found out he was a pretty righteous dude. But that was just me being me. That's all I could do. If the guy hadn't hurt anyone or anything like that, why kill him? We might have made good friends.

With only one bullet left, I knew that this had to be the one. Rob approached me again. The guy was fucking fearless. I stepped toward him and fired my final shot, just grazing the left side of his skinny neck. Dropping his knife and falling to his knees, Rob was utterly stunned. He repeatedly touched his right hand to the hole in his neck, then looked at his hand, then at me, then he repeated the process over and over again. The bloodstains grew bigger. Over and over he did this as though it was never supposed to happen to him, but it did. The blood was spilling out rapidly.

"You shot me you fuck!" Rob cried out, looking helplessly at Bob Beamer. "I'm fucking bleeding over here!" Beamer's expression was one of such fear that I sensed he had probably shit his britches.

"Can you fucking believe this? I'm gonna have a fucking scar!" Rob cried.

"Bleedin like a stuck pig, too," I added.

"I don't even know what that means, you fucking hillbilly!"

Rob sneered at me as if I were amused by his injury – which, of course, I was.

"Are you fucking crazy, asshole?" he screamed. I didn't answer because I didn't need to. Rob looked at Bob Beamer.

"What in the fuck is going on here?"

Bob Beamer had no answer for his wounded companion, and if he did, he wasn't about to offer it to Rob. He just looked at me and politely said, "I'm sorry mister, but I think we got us the wrong room."

"I forgive you. These things happen sometimes. Thanks for apologizing, too," I answered, feeling a bit sorry for Bob Beamer, messing-up his pants and all. Grabbing a tight handful of long, black curly locks, I picked up the head from the floor, and handed it to Bob Beamer. "You two jackasses get the hell outta here and take this piece of shit with you." They left without saying another word. Their exit was almost pathetically shameful. How ironical.

I yawned deep with a skyward stretch and climbed back into bed. Just before I climbed out of the dream, it hit me, and I felt deep regret for not having asked either Rob or Bob if they knew why Randy Quaid was in town.

clint

At nine-thirty a.m., I walked across the street to Clint's office. I figured since his quitting time was thirty minutes less than normal, his starting time was most likely the same. It was. Clint was a big country boy, quiet and well groomed. And that was his real name. A cowboy named Clint. I loved it.

I introduced myself and shook his hand. We had only communicated by phone and mail to that point. He asked me to sit and I did. When my ass hit the chair, it felt as though I'd sat on a cone of broken glass. He noticed that I sighed and asked if I was all right.

"Everything's wonderful except my ass."

"Got ya a case of roids do ya?"

"Yeah. I reckon the drive in got to me." I knew that wasn't it. I knew it was a direct result of the surgery. Ask any Caesarean mother on the planet. She'll tell you. I didn't really get it. They cut through your abdominal wall and your ass flares up. What happens when they cut through your ass?

"You need to get some of them... what do they call them things? Suppositories. Yeah, get you a box of them."

"Reckon I will if things don't settle down back there. I'm in denial right now – a habit I can't seem to shake."

"Understood."

Clint opened a file full of papers. To this point, we had done everything via mail, fax, and wire transfers, but now it was time to sign in black ink. I signed page after page and didn't read a word. It didn't really matter. Paper fades just like the dead.

Clint told me that the ranch I bought didn't have a registered name. He asked if I wanted to leave it that way or change it.

"Change it."

"What do you want to call it?"

"Rancho No Pescado."

"I like that, but there's two spring-fed tanks on the property, and I'm pretty sure there's still fish in em."

"That's fine, but I won't be doing any fishing." It hurt to say, but I said it. "My fishing days are done."

"Rancho No Pescado it is." He turned to the keyboard of his computer and punched in the new name wherever it applied and printed some more documents that I signed. Then he handed me the keys. Fucking keys.

"How come there's two?"

"One for the gate. One for the house." I could see he sensed that I was bothered by having two keys. "You're not gonna need em once you're down there. We just like to keep the vacant properties locked up to dissuade poachers and wets running drugs. Once you're livin down there, you'll forget about keys."

He gave me a map with directions to the property and a topographical map of the land. It was just over forty thousand acres of desert and mountains. From Marfa, it was fifty-five miles of paved highway to the ranch entrance. From there, it was twenty-five miles of dirt road to the old house.

I asked Clint if he wouldn't mind escorting me down the first time. He said he fully intended to. I told him I needed to check out of the hotel, run a few errands and I'd be ready in about an hour. We agreed to meet back at his office at noon.

As I got up to leave, a young woman walked in and smiled at me. "Hey honey," she said to Clint.

"Tami Joe!" Clint said. "This is Miles Jax. Miles, this is my wife, Tami Joe."

Tami Joe was polite and pretty and shook my hand firmly. "I've been wanting to meet you ever since I read your book. It gave me nightmares for weeks."

"That's very kind of you to say."

"Are you gonna write another?"

"Right now I'm thinking of writing one called *Wrath of a Swollen Ass*."

"He's got hemorrhoids, honey," Clint said, smiling.

"Well, if you need any help with that subject, you just let me know. With two little ones, I can tell you all about it."

"I'll keep that in mind." I shook her hand again. "It was my pleasure to meet you."

...

I walked back to the hotel, pulled myself up the stairs, entered my room, vomited bloody bile in the sink and poured myself a stiff scotch. On the balcony, I sat in a white metal chair and looked up at the great sky. In an effort to find absolute stillness I peered deep into the blue above me. *Deep. Deeper. Deeper now. Search for the end. Find the edge where the angels sing to the passersby.* What will happen to this old bag of bones? Guy Clark said they weren't really him. Are they really me? I wondered. Or are they just dust fed by blood, bound by skin, enslaved to muscle? I couldn't see life ever ending. It was too strong. It was too confusing. It was too incomplete. My quiescence took me away on a flight of wonder. It allowed my mind to hear the thoughts of my soul. That is where the life we know carries on without us, but there is something behind the songs of the angels. Notes meant for the stars of the night, the beings within, leaving behind all that will become dust. Because, in time, it will all turn to dust. There is no other option.

After checking out of the hotel, I went to the post office to get my key for my new box. Box 1895. That's me. I opened the box and found a single slip of yellow paper. It was a notice that I had received something too big to fit in my box.

"Box 1895 please sir." I handed the notice to the postmaster. He put it in a tray with the other yellow notices and went to the back. He returned with a box no bigger than one made for ladies shoes. I thanked him and went out to the Scout and tore away the wrapping. Inside was a flexible plastic envelope folded over and over again and taped tight with gray duct tape. Also in the box was an envelope with Finkel's name and address engraved in the corner. Handwritten in the middle was my name, Miles.

The envelope was not sealed. I pulled the letter and read it:

Miles, be careful. You're wanted. They don't give a shit how sick you are. They're pissed because you shit on them. I thought it was kind of funny myself.
All arrangements have been made according to your requests. And though you didn't ask for it, being the saint that I am, I decided to include you, too, in the payout.
Good luck to you my friend.
Remember, miracles happen. Farewell, Finkel

I drove to Livingston's – a combination feed store, dry goods market, boot store and gun shop. The building was old with twenty-foot high ceilings, time-worn wood floors and antique cash register made of heavy metal and glass. There was something about the place, something old and pure and honest – whatever it was lit a fire under my already inflamed ass and I went on a shopping spree like never before. I bought two shotguns – a twenty-gauge and a twelve-gauge, four cases of shotgun shells, a large skinning knife with a serrated edge at the base, a pickaxe, two shovels, a metal sign reading *TRESPASSERS WILL BE SHOT*, four cedar posts, rope, a roll of bailing wire, a pair of linesman pliers, a twenty-gallon red plastic gas can, a swing axe, a wood splitter and the biggest, baddest chainsaw in Presidio County. From there, I drove to a gas station and topped-off both the Scout and the gas can, then met Clint back at his office.

I followed behind Clint's truck for over an hour. The landscape was beautiful, the air thin and clean. Soon the mountains in the distance were at my fingertips. Maybe I was wanted, but I had never felt so free. A two-car funeral. Any more would've ruined it all.

It took another three hours before we reached the house. It was a small adobe home perched on a hill with a grand view of the Chinati Mountains. Excluding the outhouse some sixty yards downhill, the house consisted of only three rooms: a rustic kitchen with a wood-burning stove, a small living room with an even smaller bedroom, both with stone fireplaces. The floor was rough concrete, the furniture minimal and rustic. As I stood in the living room, I was besieged by a vision of the old man lying dead on the floor.

"Is this where it happened?" I asked.

"Your grandfather?"

"Yeah."

"Yes sir," he said. "This is the very room."

"Do you know where he's buried?"

"He's buried at a place he called Azle's Point. They say it was his favorite spot on the ranch. He'd go there in the evenings and watch the sun set behind Mount Francis."

"Mount Francis?"

"A mountain out yonder named after my grandmother."

"She's got herself a dang ole mountain does she? That's somethin else."

"I reckon."

"This Azle's Point, will you take me there?"

We drove in Clint's truck to Azle's Point. It was at the top of a rocky road that rolled up and down over the hills. I stepped out of the truck and looked around. The view captivated me. In every direction, I could see nothing but country. Hard, beautiful country.

"Where's he buried?"

"Right up yonder."

He pointed to a small knoll just west of us. It stood no more than thirty feet high. At the top was a swing. As we reached the top, I couldn't stop looking at the old weathered swing. It was made of eight-foot-long cedar posts with a seat built back to back. One could sit on one side and see the mountains of Mexico or sit on the other side and watch the sun slip behind the Chinatis.

"Your grandfather built this swing. It's an amazing design, really. He liked to be comfortable when he was here. I heard he'd watch the sunset, then move to the other side and watch the stars come out. I heard he slept out here on many a night – him on one side, his dogs on the other."

"How do you know so much about him?"

"He worked for my grandfather through his teens and early twenties. They say he never spent a dime of his wages. He was saving it to buy this land, and that's what he did." Clint kicked some rocks around with his head down, then looked at me. "This place has been vacant since 1972. It was bequeathed to his daughters, but they sold it immediately. Why didn't they keep it? Never mind, it's not my business. Your granddad done real well here, but I'm probably telling you things that you already know."

"No, you're not. All I know is that he was a man who lived his life's natural passion and, because of it, he lies here under a blanket of rocks."

"He was a helluva cowboy. Helluva man. You never knew him?"

"I remember sitting in his lap by the campfire. He told me stories that I can't recall. But I do remember he always seemed bigger than life. His hands were red and scarred and swollen and felt like tree bark." I thought of not answering his other questions, but I did. "My family sold for money. Money that went as fast as the memory of these old bones in the ground."

"Are they excited about you buying back the place?"

"I don't know. I don't care."

I bent to my knees and brushed away the dust and sand that covered his marker. It was a piece of native limestone laid level in the ground. Hand-chiseled into the stone was the following inscription:

John J. Jax
WWI
Cowboy
1895-1972

"Who carved the inscription?"

"I heard that his ranch foreman did it. A man by the name of Felix, I believe. When your grandmother died around 1955, he took her body back to Chihuahua City to be buried next to her parents. Your mother and aunt and uncle moved away a few years later, but he wouldn't go. Supposedly, he never saw the sense in leaving off to some place other than home. And this was his home. He ranched hard and did pretty good for himself, but no one in the family ever returned. Not until now."

"And the foreman, what happened to him?

"Your granddad had left Felix, that was his name I believe, some money to keep the place up, but he never made it that far."

"He left, too?"

"You really don't know what happened, do you?"

"Only that Pop was murdered. That's all my family ever told me."

"It seems Mr. Jax here had hired on some extra hands through some of Felix's connections in Mexico. They were going to build a new corral, install several miles of new fence line and raise a new barn with bigger stalls for his quarter horses."

"Didn't we pass all that stuff on the way up here?"

"Yeah. They got it all done, and he paid em all a real good wage. On the weekends, he'd gather em all up for a fiesta.

He did that quite a bit. They'd slaughter a steer or a pig and roast em on the spit. They played gitar and sang and drank peach brandy given to your granddad as a youngster by Milton Faver over at the Cibolo Creek Ranch. Your granddad had gone inside the house to stoke the fire. When he turned around, one of the wets shot him between the eyes."

"Why'd he do it?"

"No one knows, really. Most folks figured since he was able to hire so many hands and keep em busy with projects that the one who shot figured there was cash in the house."

"Was the cash there?"

"Yeah, twelve dollars. They tore the place apart looking for more, but there weren't none."

"What happened to the fuck that shot him?"

"He took the twelve dollars, a trailer load of your granddad's horses, his truck and disappeared into Mexico." Clint looked off at the Chinatis. "Lots of folks think this place is hexed, haunted by angry spirits. They call it Casa del Muerto."

"I like it, but you said he was a good man?"

"Your pop was, but when Felix went in and found his body, he was overcome with guilt. He dug this here grave and buried your granddad – then he walked down into that canyon yonder and shot himself right through the ear."

"He buried out here, too?"

"No. His family took him back to Mexico. Grounded em there."

"I appreciate you telling me all that. Though it's not a very pretty story."

"Yeah, I reckon the truth rarely is."

That night, I built a large fire in the stone fireplace, drank scotch, dripped morphine and fell asleep in my camouflage overalls with my bare feet warmed by the flames.

My first week at Rancho No Pescado was quite relaxing. Other than cutting wood for the fire and shooting a few scaled quail, my mission was to heal from the surgery, at least to the point that I could do what needed to be done. It gets cold in the high desert – real fucking cold. I was still in Texas, but after sundown, the temperature would drop an average of 30 degrees every evening. But I had been cold ever since the surgery – real fucking cold. I would sweat beneath the sheets, soaking myself in wet clothes, yet I couldn't get enough blankets over me to stop the shivering. Life was so strange. I swear.

Mostly, I needed stillness. I needed quiet, time to let the hands of nature work after my surrender. I needed the warmth of the fire, cold night air, light blued by the moon, silence only the land of little water can bring. It was almost easy to rest. The world and all of its belongings were gone. There was never the sound of another human voice. There was no phone or television. There was nothing, and the nothing was wonderful. It swallowed me and flew me away.

I had been back to town only once. I bought food and scotch, all the scotch, all three bottles. For the first time in my life, I felt I'd bought too much alcohol. It's strange that something like that reinforced the imminence of my death. Budgeting for my trip to the new world.

At the post office, I picked up another package from Finkel. It contained a hand-written note from him, another wad of cash, some legal documents, including my will, and others about my book. They were going forward with it "with great enthusiasm." Of course they were. Even if it was shit, they'd still publish it. No one sells books better than a dead man.

It's easy for artists to convert their work from contemporary to classic. All they have to do is die.

I signed the will, mailed it back to Chicago, stuffed the cash in my pocket and drove back to Rancho No Pescado.

At the end of my first week, I sat in front of the fireplace and watched the empty bag of morphine melt away. Using my knife and pliers, I plucked away the staples from my incision. It was essentially painless, but the incision was red, either infected or irritated by the extended stay of the staples – turned out to be both.

Above the fireplace was an old Mexican mirror. The glass was water-stained and coated with years of dust. The frame was ornately carved mahogany, dusty and cracking from years in the dry desert air. It was a beautiful piece, and though I didn't know the history behind it, I imagined my grandfather appreciating its splendor when he first hung it.

I stood and looked into the mirror as I thought he would have, but, through the dust and years of loneliness, came an unwanted image. I could count my ribs. All of my body fat was gone. My eyes were bloodshot and still the color of rain clouds in the sun. The blue was gone. So was the pretty that Lauren saw. It was the simple reflection of physical failure blossoming.

I sat down in a wood chair with my face in the palms of my hands. I could feel the pounding infection in my hand where I had pulled the heplock. It had become red and bruised and swollen with infection. Before the doubt could surface, I spoke aloud the words of Helen Keller.

"I am never discouraged by absence of good. I never can be argued into hopelessness. Doubt and mistrust are the mere panic of timid imagination, which the steadfast heart will conquer, and the large mind transcend."

With that, I walked out of the house. It was another cold night, and the wind blew in steady out of the northwest beneath a cloudless sky of stars. At a rock water trough fed by a natural spring just uphill, I splashed virgin water over my incision and scrubbed away the dried crusts of blood. With no fat tissue left on my body, my muscle tissue was rapidly degrading. I could feel the failing organs in my abdomen pulsating – limp and tired but still fighting against the disease that I had allowed to ravage them so.

I rinsed my face and hair and washed the grime of illness from my body. At the flow pipe, I cupped my hands and drank water fresh from the earth. The water was warm and pure. I was the first human to touch it, and I could taste its fresh beauty. It could only help me. I drank until I could drink no more. Then vomited. Then drank more and walked back toward the house.

Inside Casa del Muerto, I toweled off and dressed in clean, warm clothes. I poured a glass of scotch and sat down in front of the fire with an orange for dinner. In the quiet and warmth and without the infusion of morphine, I found a space in which I could finally think. I closed my eyes and slowed my breathing. What will it be like when I die? What will become of the world? What will become of me? The more I thought of it, the clearer it became, and any fears I had been harboring dissolved into nonexistence. There was only peace. It was well-defined but boundless and silently spoke to me of only good things. And with the undertow of Mud Cut sucking at my feet, I released myself to it and sailed through a place that was without sickness or hatred or indifference. There were no colors or sounds or separations, and it was okay. I opened my eyes to the flaming mesquite, drank from my glass and smiled in the silence of the desert night.

Opening the envelope from Finkel, I read his note:

Miles,
Your friend, James Jonas, is dead.
They say he resisted arrest in Arizona.
He was shot three times in the back.
I don't know what's going on, but watch your ass.
So long friend,
Finkel
– please start a fire with this

I dropped the note into the flames. Outside I fell to my knees, vomiting a watery muddle of orange pulp. My eyes welled with tears. The withered muscles of my stomach burned with each wrenching. When it was over, I stayed curled on the ground crying out for mercy for the man I had killed.

"Forgive me, James Jonas."

As though he heard my words, I felt the fall of light rain on my neck. I rolled over onto my back and cried as the rain came down in a steady quiet drizzle. I knew where James Jonas was. I knew he felt the water flowing inside him. I knew he understood. But his daughter, she would know nothing, and that hurt me.

"Don't fucking move."

The voice above me had a heavy Mexican accent. Rough. Firm. Determined. He sat the barrel of his gun down on my forehead. I did not move. He spoke again, but thunder rumbled and broke in the canyon. It boomed loud, and I thought for an instant that I was dead, but the gun lay still on my skin, and the rain came down heavy.

"Are you Miles Jax?"

"Fuck you." I pushed the gun away and stood up. I looked at the man, the barrel of his .357 stuck in my face. "I'm going inside. You're welcome to come in."

I grabbed four cut pieces of mesquite and walked inside the house. The man said nothing, but I could feel him lurking behind me. I didn't know if he'd kill me or not, and I didn't really care. To me, there was no difference. I'd been to the place where there are no droppings of humanity. I liked it there. If I showed up early, so be it.

Inside, I added one log to the fire and set the others aside. I went about my business, with the Mexican and his gun behind me. Do me the fucking favor, I thought.

I got a second glass and poured both half full, took one to the stranger threatening to shoot me, then stripped bare, hanging my wet clothes on either side of the rock mantle. I pulled another chair by the fire then sat in my chair, sipped my scotch and stoked the fire.

"You can see I'm unarmed, and we're not going anywhere for a while, so how boutcha?"

He said nothing as he sat down, the gun resting in my direction. Brilliant flashes of light struck silently through the window. Thunder rolled and roared in the canyon. The lamp, my only light, went out. It was the fuse at the pole behind the house, but I didn't say anything. A strong wind earlier in the week had caused the electricity to go out, but I hadn't realized it was the outside fuses until the next day. I'd put the ice trays outside and lit a honeysuckle-scented candle that reminded me of the swampy deep south. I slept well that night. No man-made power. Nothing but flame and a night cold and quiet. It was quite pleasant.

"Blaze Foley said, 'Love – nothing else like it around.' What do you think?"

"I think you are not well in your head. This is what I think."

I looked at him in the burn of the firelight. He was a short, fat man. His round face was rough but held the natural look of a jolly man. His balding hair a shaggy gray and black.

"The head you were just about to blow to pieces?" I asked.

"Yes. That head. And I still might if you think you're getting out of this one."

"Mister, I am forced to use my time wisely. Please don't think that I doubt your abilities or determination. That was not my intention." I eyed his glass. "You ought to drink that scotch. It tastes better that a way."

I sat with the man and sipped my scotch. The fire was lovely, brilliant dancing flames, warmth, natural and scented, rushing over me. When the man raised his glass, I closed my eyes and drifted away in the rising heat.

Let the whiskey burn sweetly on his tongue. Let it fall down inside and warm him. Let him think of who he is. Let him drift inward into the peace that waits just beyond our reach. Let him know what it is that matters, and let the silence be blown away with the action of his weapon. And when I fall, the glass will break – the whiskey and blood will come together outside the body where they will find no more use for their blend. Waste in waste and nothing to come but decay and memories soon to be forgotten.

When I opened my eyes, the man was just finishing his drink. I held out the bottle and refilled his glass, then poured a bit more in mine.

"You think I'm sick in the head?"

"From what I've seen so far I can think nothing else."

"How long have you been watching me?"

"Three days."

"Are you a police officer?"

"They call what I do bounty hunting."

"There's a price on my head?"

"Yes."

"How much?"

"Five thousand dollars."

"Five grand for a broken head. What do the good ones go for?"

The man looked at me and said nothing. Then he smiled and giggled without sound. For a quick moment, we laughed together.

"How old are you?" I asked.

"Why?"

"Curious."

"I'm old."

"Fifty-seven?"

"Sixty-two."

"You're sixty-two and chasing crazy people through the desert?"

"Yes."

"Are you broke?"

"No."

"Lonely?"

"No."

"Then you love your work?"

"I do."

"You're a lucky man. What's your name?"

"This is not necessary for you to know my name."

"You know mine."

"Yes, I know your name, Mr. Jax. It is my job to know this."

"You're right, Stanley, it is your..."

"What did you call my name?"

"I didn't call your name anything. I simply referred to you as Stanley because I refuse to sit in my own fucking house and converse with a man pointing a fucking gun at me and not have the slightest idea of what his fucking name is."

"Why this Stanley?"

"Stanley was my first dog, a Boxer. He used to stand in the middle of the street and wait for cars. They'd stop, and Stanley would chew on their tires. Most of his teeth were broken but he never got run over. One day he lay down in the back yard and died."

"How old was he?"

"Old."

"I remind you of this dog?"

"Just in the face."

I smiled at Stanley and we laughed together. I liked Stanley.

"My name is Ernesto."

As the storm raged outside, I looked at Ernesto in the firelight and thanked him. He holstered his gun and put another log on the fire. I filled our glasses, and the rain came down. It was a lovely evening.

"Have you always known what you were meant to do?" I asked.

"What do you mean?"

"I mean have you always felt certain that your life was going down the path which God intended it to travel?"

"I have no regrets. I have a large family. My children are good. Their children are good. Law has always been my passion. I was a police officer in San Antonio for nearly thirty years. Before that, I fought in Korea."

"Inchon?"

"Yes. MacArthur."

"Do you ever wonder why it was you that lived the life you lived and not someone else's?"

"I don't understand."

"Ernesto, I don't either. Sometimes I wonder why I was so damn lucky. There's folks out there with nothing. Not food. Not water. It just doesn't seem fair."

We drank more, and I vomited in the ash bucket. Afterwards, I shivered uncontrollably. Ernesto added wood to the fire as I slipped into my camouflage overalls. I wore my hunting hat with the ear flaps down to conserve body heat. The rain kept coming, but the fire was alive and dancing, and, as I warmed, we fell back into a comfortable glaze of conversation – that old man and me.

Ernesto knew a lot about me. He knew I was a fugitive, a narcotics thief, a loner, a drunk and drug addict. He also knew I was another paycheck. But not until he saw my physical state did he realize that I was holding onto life by the strand of a feather. He knew I was no threat to him, and I knew I had chosen not to be one. Had I resisted his efforts, he would've been forced to take me back without hesitation, and that was not an option for me. I had left that world behind, and I was not going back only to die in it.

"You wouldn't happen to have any marijuana on you, would you?"

He didn't answer.

"Yeah, it helps me dream. For some time now, a child has been beckoning me back to him, but ever since I've moved here my sleep is black and dreamless."

"Maybe you are too drunk to remember any dreams."

"That's thoughtful of you to say, Ernesto, but I don't think that's it. I've always been a dreamer."

"Have they come true, your dreams?"

"All but one."

I sat my glass on the concrete floor then lay down next to it, resting my head on a cold wet boot. I closed my eyes and the firelight jumped through my darkness. The rain fell heavy on the old tin roof, and the thunder shook and raged in the canyon. It was God playing Mozart's "Requiem," and I slipped into the black as Ernesto fruitlessly asked me about the one.

azle's point

At Azle's Point the ground was well-soaked. The earth gave
way easily to the shovel, but each load was wet heavy and
difficult to lift. The rocks were endless as I dug. Using a
pickaxe and a heavy rock bar to loosen them, I tossed them
out with my bare frozen hands.

I had left Casa del Muerto quietly in the middle of the night,
leaving behind my gloves and any food or water. The rains
had fallen back to a steady drizzle, but the thunder still
growled, and each strike of lightning lit up the mountains of
Mexico in the southern distance. I shivered uncontrollably as
I dug, but I kept digging, knowing it would be only shortly
after dawn when Ernesto would simply follow the tire ruts
that would lead him right to me.

With the desert ground being what it was – sand, rock, cactus
and mesquite root – the rain was a flowing sanction. And to
think I was going to do this on a dry day. That alone would
most likely have killed me.

The trench I had dug was much smaller than what I'd
originally hoped. Plans changed as I grew weaker and spilled
my bloody illness on the broken ground. After four hours of
steady digging, I had a trench some seven feet long, two feet
wide and barely three feet deep. This was all that I could
handle. At three feet the earth was too solid for me to break.
It would have to do. Hopefully the rocks would stave off the
hogs and coyotes. Hopefully someone would put them there.
It would probably be poor old Ernesto. That seemed sort of
unfair, but so goes life.

I sat on the edge of the trench with my feet resting in the hole
and watched the sky wreak a glorious life of chaos over the
earth. Soon snow mixed with the rain, and, off to the
southeast, I could sense the day coming. A strip of lighter
darkness fell like a white ribbon over the earth. It stretched

the length of the entire horizon and draped shyly on the great plateaus, portending a new life yet to come. Never before had I seen so far, not even at night on the ocean. The world reached out forever, and nothing but earth and animal noticed. And I wondered then what it was that *I* ever did to J.D. Salinger.

An hour before daybreak, I walked back down the hill to the old Scout and retrieved a heavy piece of limestone, a chisel and a mallet. The stone I had found on my third day at Rancho No Pescado. I was walking the rim of Round Rock Canyon, a deep and jagged drop about an hour's drive northwest of Casa del Muerto. There at the tip of a platform of jutting rock was the perfect stone, slightly concave and severed somehow by nature – eroded by drought and sunlight and wind, sucked of all its life by the needs of the high desert and disregarded as waste. Or it might have given way to the pressure of the great phantom Mule buck and snapped under his silent might. It was as though I was being surprised with an unexpected gift that I immediately knew I would love.

Back at the trench, I set the stone in the ground and began to chisel. It was rough going all the way through. My hands were blue and bleeding beneath a heavy coat of soil. Several times I missed the chisel and slammed the mallet hard into my knuckles. And though I knew I had broken my thumb, the pain was essentially buried beneath the cold, the rain and the damn blood. Pain was just a word by default, but cold and weakness and death – these were now more than just words. They were feelings, strange and coming, moving down from the mountain slopes to find me in solemn anguish working for their cause.

When I could no longer chisel, I set aside the tools and tipped the stone up to drain the rainwater pooling on its surface. The markings were legible, but the craftsmanship was poor. With more time, it would have been much more pleasant to the eye, but that was not to be. With numb hands, blue and dirty and bleeding, I scooped away the slop soil and set the stone.

Pushing mud and rock snug to the sides of the stone helped to anchor it in place. Rainwater began to gather at its center. It would stay if the storm let up by noon. If not, maybe my child would find it one day and bring it back to me. And just as those of old did no more date the life of the living with days and months, so did I date only the years. Did they do it because there were no records? Could no one remember? Did they just want to die? Did it really matter? Then, I realized that it was always the headstones that listed only the years that drew me to them. In pictures, I remembered them. At funerals I stood by them and wondered. Now I knew. It didn't matter.

I took my seat at the back of the trench, my feet resting heavy on the bottom. The rain was still coming, and the snow began to fall steady. It was soft and oddly warm on my hands.

I thought of men who lived short lives. I thought of men who lived long lives. But I thought more of the men who gave something wonderful to the world with whatever life they lived. I admired these men. I wondered why they did it, and I did not. Maybe it's the hoops of humility through which these people have to jump. It must have been numbing to sincerity. Scars of war. It's true that the only free thing in this world is nothing. You may have all of it you want. The chase is for something. Nothing is simply abandoned for those like me. It grows in great abundance and feeds lost souls the accoutrements they need to go on without being people of merit or prominence. But what of all the happiness and the absence of mankind spewing its furious charge in our faces? Is it not deserved? Oh, but I imagined that indeed it was. And with the rest of humanity running away, we, the simple outcasts of society are left behind to soak in the ocean of hidden meaning and traverse the obscure oddities of life until such time as we are no longer needed here. And that time seems most untimely, but we are not the keepers of the clock, only its conjectured scholars.

The rain relented, and the snow fell hard in its place. The horizon broke with soft white light, revealing a thorny desert coated in cotton. It was a majestic sight, and with night falling away, the winds of morning blew strong. So glorious was it that I was no longer shivering. Stillness and warmth had found me perched solemnly on Azle's Point, watching the greasewood sway and the cholla stocks gather fresh fallen snow.

But the world was not mine alone for long. I saw dark, quiet movement in the brush. Looking closer, I saw it again. Like madness striking me from behind, I leapt to my feet and ran down the slope into the brush. Stopping just ahead of where I had marked the movement, I stood waiting next to a mesquite tree. Through the wind-driven sheets of snow stepped an old Mexican man. His expression sad, his face darkly creased and weathered hard, the pupils of his eyes broken by a life of poverty, hard work and gloom.

He came to me as if to surrender, but I held out my hand for him to shake. At first he hesitated, then took my swollen hand into his. Behind him emerged a Mexican woman, aged and wrinkled – my grandmother's Indian blanket warming her and the small child that she held in her arms. Neither said a word to me, and I could only look at them and marvel. They had nothing but the tethered clothes on their backs, but to me they had almost everything.

I removed my boots and socks and handed them to the old man. I knew they were not his size, but he was in no position to question and he reluctantly accepted. Then I stripped the overalls from my body, retrieved from the pocket a cash-filled envelope marked "Ernesto" and surrendered both the clothing and money to him. We all stood for a moment in silence, then I smiled at them and spoke the only Spanish that I knew. "Vaya con Dios."

As I turned to walk away, I felt a warm hand on my shoulder. The old woman held the small child in one arm and moved her hand from my shoulder to my forehead. She closed her black eyes and chanted softly, slowly lowering her hand over my eyes, closing them, then resting her warm hand over my heart. It was the tongue of a bruja, and I fell away in words I knew not, but felt like fiery blessings burning inside me.

When she lifted her hand, I opened my eyes to nothing but snowfall. Both she and the old man and the child had vanished into the white desert. The earth was silent. Its vast distances had closed in, and I could see everything in the world and beyond. For a moment I stood motionless and watched everything be – be as it may. Be as it will. Be as God made it.

Walking back up to Azle's Point was a stroll through the ethereal wonderment of life, a walk through the ever-so-clear equinox of human existence. Beneath my feet, the stone and thorn were without malice, the wind thoughtfully at my back, and the silence, the final drop of Mozart's hands.

Inside the trench, I knelt and looked at the limestone. The snow had dissolved quite precisely in the fresh inscription. It read:

M J Jax
1963 – 1996
fisherman

Looking out again, I saw Paul playing in the snow. He said nothing to me. I lay down in the trench and closed my eyes. I never heard another sound. I never needed to.

www.ingramcontent.com/pod-product-compliance
Lightning Source LLC
Chambersburg PA
CBHW030336030726
47499CB00003B/798